Samko Tále's Cemetery Book

by the same author

1926–1996 (*short story*), Poviedka '96

Keep it in the Family (Nech to zostane to v rodine), Anasoft litera 2005

Murder in Slopná (Vražda v Slopnej), Slovart 2007

Daniela Kapitáňová

Samko Tále's Cemetery Book

translated by Julia Sherwood

GARNETT PRESS

LONDON

first published in Great Britain in 2011 by
The Garnett Press,
Dpt of Russian (SML)
Queen Mary (University of London),
Mile End Road, London E1 4NS

ISBN 978-0-9535878-9-6

Introduction

DANIELA KAPITÁŇOVÁ was born on 30 July 1956 in Komárno, a Slovak town on the Danube, opposite the Hungarian city of Komárom. She has come to fiction fairly late in life. She trained as a theatre director in Prague, and directed in both Slovak and Czech theatres. She works for Slovak Radio, writes opinion pieces and teaches creative writing at the University of Constantine the Philosopher in Nitra.

In 1996 she entered a short-story competition: her entry *1926–1996* won first prize and publishers' interest. *Samko Tále's Cemetery Book* came four years later, under the pseudonym of the narrator, Samko Tále, an intellectually and physically stunted creature and arch-conformist who enthusiastically embraces every kind of prejudice under Communism and as it continued in the newly independent Slovakia. This book was a sensation when it appeared in 2000; still a best-seller in its fourth edition, it has been compared to *Forrest Gump*, and Samko Tále was seen as a reincarnation of Oskar Matzerath in *The Tin Drum* or Holden Caulfield in *The Catcher in the Rye* — in fact he is a genuinely original creation, who is gradually revealed as reflecting the worst in human nature. *Samko Tále's Cemetery Book* has been translated into Czech, Swedish, French, German, Arabic, Polish and Japanese and now appears in English.

Since then, Daniela Kapitáňová has switched to what may seem at first sight to be pastiches of Agatha Christie and other traditional detective novels. Her second novel, *Keep it in the Family* (Nech to zostane v rodine, 2005), begins with the acerbic irony of Muriel Spark, before reaching its conclusion through an interrogation by the Slovak equivalent of Hercule Poirot. In 2007 she published *Murder in Slopná* (Vražda v Slopnej), where virtually all the detectives of European fiction descend on the case, each reaching their own conclusions.

Daniela Kapitáňová has, like Muriel Spark, an acerbic black humour. She has little time for local nationalism, or the new Europhile materialism, and is impatient with critics and readers who cling to romantic ideals. Her work introduces an ironic, but liberal (and quietly feminist) streak into Slovakia's stream of thought. One of her comments is particularly telling: 'What I have in mind is art produced by specific individuals, which shapes the cultural awareness of a nation. This is what determines what is generally believed to express how we feel about life. [...] It is very hard to accelerate cultural progress. It is much, much easier to replace an outdoor privy with a flushing toilet.'

Some guidance for the British reader…

Time and place
The novel is set in the mid-1990s, a few years after Slovakia has been 'divorced' by the Czech Republic, but while memories of the Communist past are still fresh, in the town of Komárno on the Danube, where Slovaks mingle, often resentfully, with Hungarians and Roma (Gypsies).

Currency
The Slovak crown was at the time worth about 45 to the pound. (In 2009 Slovakia adopted the euro).

Spartakiad
Mass gymnastics event regularly held in Communist Czechoslovakia

Some characters and how to pronounce their names
We have decided to keep Slovak spellings of characters' names, but here is a guide to pronouncing the more problematic ones. All names are stressed on the first syllable:

Samko Tále	*pronounce as*	Samko Tahley
Ján Boš-Mojš		Yahn Bosh-Moish
Alf. Névéry		Alf Nayvayri
Eszter Csonka		Ester Chonka
Zoltán Csipke		Zoltahn Chipke
Žebrák		Zh [*s as in leisure*]ebrahk
Osladičová		Osladichova
Ľudovít Bucz		Lyudoveet Boots
Katuša Szedíleková		Katoosha Sedeelekova

In Slovak, a woman or a girl has the suffix -ová added to the surname of her husband or father.

Kezét csókolom is a Hungarian greeting that roughly translates as *I kiss your hand.* Its equivalents in Slovak (*Ruky bozkávam*) and German (*Küss die Hand*) were widely used in countries of the former Austro-Hungarian Empire.

Julia Sherwood and Donald Rayfield

The First Cemetery Book.

In Komárno there is a Cemetery. It is very nice. It is big and spacious. It has a lot of graves. The graves are very nice. They're laid out in rows. Or not, sometimes. There are gravestones and crosses. They've got names on them.

People go to the Cemetery. Some go in the morning and others in the afternoon. Some people bring little rakes. And whatever.

The Cemetery has two gates. One is for people and the other is for corpses. Corpses are dead people what have died. They're in the mortuary. A mortuary's a building meant for corpses. Outside the mortuary there's a courtyard. There are often funerals in the courtyard. It's very nice.

There are people who work at the Cemetery. They're very nice and like to help other people. They dig holes and look after them. They wear suits. The suits are very nice. In the winter the Cemetery is cold. In the summer it is hot. In the spring the cemetery comes to life.

Lots of funny things and sad things can happen at the Cemetery.

I don't know what else to write about the Cemetery.

It's very nice.

Samko Tále. Writer.
Komárno.

The Second Cemetery Book

This is the second time I've become a writer because I've already been a writer once. That time I wrote the first Cemetery Book. Today I've become a writer again because it's raining, and when it's raining I can't collect cardboard, because it's raining. But the most important thing is that my handcart is in the workshop, because my rear-view mirror has been broken off, and I don't know how to fix it because you need special tools or whatever to fix it and I can't do that, because I haven't got them. My rear-view mirror has never ever been broken off before, though I've had my handcart for twenty-eight years, because I'm hard-working and people respect me for being hard-working.

The workshop is on the Island and it's got special tools. The man who fixes things with his special tools is called Ján Boš-Mojš and the funny thing about him is that every time he says his name, Ján Boš-Mojš, he doesn't say it, he sort of sings it like this: Ján Boš-Mojš. He sings his name to a sort of Ján Boš-Mojš tune. But apart from that he is hard-working and people respect him, because he has a son who is very ill with elypsy, and Ján Boš-Mojš has to look after him because elypsy is the sort of illness where you have to be looked after.

His son's name is Ján Boš-Mojš Junior.

They're both in my notebook, because I have three notebooks. One is called Christian Names, the other one is called Surnames and the third one is called Died. That's where I write down everyone I know, because if I didn't write down everyone I know, how would I know who I know, right?

Right.

I've got Ján Boš-Mojš and Ján Boš-Mojš Junior in my Surnames notebook down under the letter B and also under the letter M, because you never know what's what and why and how.

Anyway.

I've got lots of first names in my Christian Names Notebook. Mostly they're Peters. I've got thirty-one Peters, except that one of them writes his name like this: Petr and that's the Czech way of writing it but I've got him down as Peter anyway because he's not a Czech, he's a Hungarian. The thing is, when he was born, the person in charge of writing people's names in the Documents left out the second E, but that was when we still had Czechoslovakia so it was OK to write it that way: Petr, but it's not

OK to write it like that now, and he'd be in big trouble for that, because in proper Slovak you have to write it like this: Peter. Or else change it.

Because that's the law.

The best time to be a writer is when it's raining because that's when I can't collect cardboard anyway because that's when that idiot Krkan from Recycling won't take it, because he says it's wet, but he will take it from other people even when it's wet, that idiot Krkan. He takes it from other people like that Gypsy rat-woman Angelika Édesová, and he takes it from her even if hers is wet. But I know what's going on. What's going on is that when that rat-woman Angelika Édesová comes in, he puts up a note saying 'Back soon', but he's never back soon, because he locks himself in the Recycling Office with that rat-woman Angelika Édesová and does sexual things with her. That's why he takes it from her even when it's wet and he won't take it from me when it's wet, but that's his problem. He'll see. He'll get reported and he'll be in big trouble for that. But I don't care, because I'm hard-working and I can always find something to do, for example now I'm a writer.

The reason why it's hard to be a writer is because it makes your hand hurt. Except that I have to be a writer because when I had my fortune told it said:

'Will write the Cemetery Book.'

It was old Gusto Rúhe who told my fortune and what he said was this: 'Will write the Cemetery Book.' But he is an alcoholic because he lives on alcohol and he smells really awful, because he often wets himself. Anyway.

He's always sitting in front of the Pub by the Railway Station and he urinates into the Floral Display, and when he tells fortunes he spits, burps and slurps all over the place because he thinks that's the law for fortune-telling.

Old Gusto Rúhe tells fortunes like this:

He tells fortunes due to a Moonstone.

Moonstone is a kind of stone that's yellow and almost transparent, because you can see right through it. Its name is Moonstone. I haven't got it down in my Surnames Notebook because it's a stone and I don't even know if that's its real name, or if old Gusto Rúhe just made it up. It's cold when you touch it. When you're having your fortune told you have to hold the Moonstone until it gets all warmed up. And then, when it's warmed up so that it's all warm, you give it back to old Gusto Rúhe. And when he's done with all his burping and whatever, he writes your fortune on the tarmac with a piece of chalk like they have at school. This is what he wrote for me:

'Will write the Cemetery Book.'

But old Gusto Rúhe is an alcoholic and he'd write any old rubbish in the world for an alcoholic drink, just to make people believe that his fortune telling is for real and to make them buy him an alcoholic drink because he is an alcoholic, even though it's not good for you and it damages your organs.

I gave him some Cat's Tongue chocolate for telling my fortune, but old Gusto Rúhe got really angry and started shouting that I would come to a bad end, and that frightened me, because even if old Gusto Rúhe is just making it up, it really happened once for real that he put a spell on Erik Rak. When I'm done writing this, I'll write about him putting a spell on Erik Rak. But because he once put a really bad spell on Erik Rak, I decided to buy him an alcoholic drink. And then old Gusto Rúhe calmed down and he was calm again. And he stopped all his burping and slurping and spitting and wrote the word Boy on the tarmac.

The thing is I hate it when people call me Boy, because I'm not a boy, I'm nearly forty-four years old and people respect me because I'm hard-working, even though I don't need to work because I have a disability pension due to my kidneys, and I have another illness as well that has a proper name, but that illness has nothing to do with my disability pension, I just have it. My disability pension has gone up quite a lot because people respect me.

Anyway.

People keep on asking me all the time to do deliveries in my handcart and when they ask me I do deliveries, even though I'm not supposed to lift heavy things, because it's very bad for me. I have to take good care regarding my health because I have a disability pension, so I have to keep healthy because if I'm not healthy I could get ill and that would be very dangerous.

That's why I have a healthy life of style and I take plenty of exercise out in the fresh air and I only have a light supper in the evening.

My hands and feet don't swell up. In wintertime I wear thermal underpants. One pair of my thermal underpants is called Panther and another one is called Trikota. The underpants called Panther have an animal called a panther embroidered on the leg. The underpants called Trikota don't have an animal embroidered on them.

People have to lift heavy things by themselves because I'm not allowed to do so by law, so I don't care, even if they beg me. When we still had the Communist Party, I was nearly the only person in Komárno doing deliveries, but now the Communist Party's gone and some shops deliver things, too. But back then it was only me and a few other people.

Another reason why some people call me Boy is because I'm not very tall because I didn't grow very much, because I have this illness that has a proper name and with this illness you never have to shave and you don't grow. But I don't need to grow anyway because I'm nearly forty-four years old and nobody in the world grows when they're nearly forty-four, right?

Right.

The thing is, even though I haven't grown like everyone else in the world, it was me they picked to recite the Young Pioneer's Oath for the whole class, because I was normal just like everyone else and I still am, because I'm no retard and I went to a normal school, not a Special School for retards, because I'm no retard. That's why I was chosen to recite the Young Pioneer's Oath.

The Young Pioneer's Oath is beautiful.

I recited the Young Pioneer's Oath on stage at the Cultural Centre in Komárno, and it was just me on my own reciting it for the whole class, and I can still remember every word of the Young Pioneer's Oath. Nobody else remembers it any more, even though they went on to lots of different schools but I do, because I remember everything, because I've got I.Q.

My Grandfather, whom we used to call Grandaddy, went with me to take the Young Pioneer's Oath because when he found out that nobody else wanted to go with me he got angry and said that the High Ups would find out and that anyone who didn't go would get into big trouble. That's why he went with me so that he wouldn't get into big trouble.

When the Young Pioneer's Oath was over, we went to a café together with Karol Gunár (PhD Social Sciences) and his daughter Darinka Gunárová.

I saw Darinka Gunárová yesterday.

Grandaddy invited us to the café, because I was the one they picked to recite the Young Pioneer's Oath, and that was a big thing, so we all went to the café and had all sorts of fizzy drinks and pastries.

But the worst problem was that my Young Pioneer's scarf wasn't really red. It was sort of orange. The good thing was that it didn't crease and its corners didn't fray. But it wasn't like all the other Young Pioneers' scarves in our class. I still have it because I keep it wrapped up in a napkin in a box and sometimes I think about it a lot. Like why it wasn't really red, but sort of orange. Then again, it didn't need ironing. But it wasn't like all the other Young Pioneer's scarves in the world.

Grandmummy said that she would make me a Young Pioneer's scarf that was really red and would crease and have corners that frayed if I wanted one, but I got frightened that Grandmummy might do something that wasn't allowed, because back then you couldn't just make your own Young Pioneer's scarf because it wasn't allowed. Because then anyone could have made themselves a Young Pioneer's scarf, or even two, and that would have been quite out of order. Because then some person who had never been a Young Pioneer in their life could have had his own Young Pioneer's scarf and that would have been a total disaster.

The thing is, Grandmummy was a tailor regarding men's clothes and that's why she thought that she was allowed to make Young Pioneers' scarves.

We used to call our grandparents Grandmummy and Grandaddy, but only at home because it would have been weird to call them Grand-mummy and Grandaddy in front of other people, because I don't know anybody else in the world or in Komárno who's called Grandmummy or Grandaddy. Because that's in German and we're in Slovakia.

But Grandmummy and Grandaddy were not German because they were in Slovakia, except that Grandmummy's grandmother was Hungarian and her name was Eszter Csonka, meaning that she had a Hungarian name too. And nobody liked that.

I didn't like it, either.

Grandmummy used to read German detective stories and she read them in German, except that she had to wrap them up in newspaper because Grandaddy was scared that they would get into trouble, because those detective stories came from a woman who had gone to Germany for emigration. The stories were called Allan Wilton. They were in magazines. They had covers too. The covers had lots of different photographs with lots of different people in them. I used to look at the photographs until Grandaddy said that they had to be wrapped up in newspaper regarding unvisibility. Grandmummy always used to tell me all about Allan Wilton and what he was up to, because he was a detective. I loved him because he always solved everything and he was very modest, too He was especially modest regarding women.

Sometimes the photos were in colour. But I couldn't understand them in colour either because I don't speak German because I don't have time for such silly things. I can speak Slovak because I'm a Slovak and I can speak Hungarian because I've learned it because I've got I.Q., even though you're not supposed to do that, because this is Slovakia.

And I also know lots of different sentences in German and Grandmummy taught me a song as well that's in German and it's about my dear friend Augustin, except that it doesn't call him my dear friend, it calls him Duleeber instead. The song goes like this:

'Oh, Duleeber Augustin, Augustin, Augustin,
Oh, Duleeber Augustin,
Alex is in.'

Meaning there's somebody with the name Augustin.

Once there was this man in Komárno whose name was Augustýn, only there wasn't just one but two of them because they were brothers and the two Augustýn brothers worked for the Customs. They had a Mum and she worked at the Post Office and when she was 47 years old, she went round the bend due to believing that all the men in Komárno were in love with her and that they only ever came to the Post Office because of her.

She always made a total disaster at the Post Office and kept saying that all those men were only there due to her, so in the end they had to move her from the Post Office counter to another office at the back of the Post Office but that didn't help at all, because she went on making a total disaster. And people made fun of her for being like that. Then her sons the young Augustýns took her out of the Post Office and she stayed at home. And then they started to go around with bicycle chains so that they could beat up anyone who made fun of her. And if anyone made fun of their Mum, one of the Augustýns would grab him and the other one would beat him up with the bicycle chain. They carried those bicycle chains in their uniform pockets.

And everyone respected them due to that.

I also respected them due to that.

Then Augustýnová the Mum died of a stroke of bad luck because she swallowed all the rings she used to wear on her fingers and by the time they found her she had gone dead.

Her name was Alenka Augustýnová.

Her sons the young Augustýns were called Tomáš and Tibor.

But they weren't the same ones as in the German song because they were quite different Augustýns.

There's just one thing I don't get and that's why old Gusto Rúhe had to write this: 'Will write the Cemetery Book', because I've no idea why I should write about the Cemetery. I've already written a book about the Cemetery once, but it was only short, just one page long, so maybe that's why it wasn't good enough and I don't even know what happened to it.

I sent it to this man, he lives in Levice and his name is Koloman Kertész Bagala, and what he does is he asks people to write lots of different books and then he collects them, but not for Recycling but so that he can make a living out of them.

He said that there was this competition and that everyone in the world could send him any book they wrote, so I thought this was a good time for me to write the Cemetery Book, so I wrote it and I sent it to him but I never heard back from him but Koloman Kertész Bagala has to write to me and tell me what's happened to my Cemetery Book because that's the law, right?

Right.

Sometimes I think that maybe he's not real or maybe he's not a man at all because at school we did this writer, her name was Timrava and she was a woman. Seriously, I'm not making it up, she was a woman and her name was Timrava not Timravaová, even though a proper Slovak name for a woman is supposed to have -ová at the end, like Darinka Gunárová, she's also called Darinka Gunárová with -ová at the end because that's the law. And that made me think that maybe this Bagala is not a man either, maybe he's a woman called Bagala, and he's just making fun of people but that's not allowed and he'll get reported and he'll be in big trouble.

The thing is, I don't want to say anything against him, because maybe my biggest mistake was that it was only one page long, because it's true that books usually have more pages, so maybe he just thought it wasn't long enough. But now Ján Boš-Mojš is mending my handcart and in addition to that it's raining outside, so I've got time to write a longer book. But there's just one thing I don't get, why it's got to be about a Cemetery? Nobody in the world can write a longer book about a Cemetery than my first Cemetery Book, because what can you write about a Cemetery, right?

Right.

Because I'm no retard, I've seen all sorts of books and I've read all sorts of books too, especially the one that was the most beautiful book in the world. It was called *The Young Pioneer's Heart* and it was about this boy who wanted to be a Young Pioneer, but the baddie wouldn't let him. That was the most beautiful book in the world and sometimes I think that no other book in the world can be more beautiful than *The Young*

Pioneer's Heart. I used to cry every time I read it but it was OK to cry then because we still had the Communist Party.

I was given *The Young Pioneer's Heart* at school because I came top at collecting waste paper and inside the book it said that it was dedicated to Samuel Tále by the Young Pioneers in honour of his outstanding achievements in collecting waste paper.

Ivana used to make fun of this book, because she's my sister and she's a great artist from Bratislava but I hate it when people laugh at things that you're not supposed to make fun of.

For example, Alf Névéry never laughed at this book, but he was very weird like that because he never laughed at anything that was funny and he always laughed at things that weren't funny at all. I don't know why he was like that, maybe because he wasn't humorous because there are people like him that aren't humorous.

But I'm very humorous.

And the way you can tell that I'm humorous is due to lots of different humorous sentences that I know. Some of them are in foreign languages too because I've got I.Q. Like in English I can say *Fuck me tender fuck me do*. That's humorous.

Or I can say 'Eins, zwei, drei, du bist arsehole'. That's humorous in German. But the most humorous sentence of all is the one this actor from the Hungarian Regional Theatre in Košice taught me. His name was Bátori and he was from Bátorove Kosihy. And the sentence goes like this:

Attention, attention, there'll be no concert, because that cunt Volodya nicked the balalaika.

This sentence is in Russian, and every time we met in the street, Bátori used to go like this:

'So is the balalaika concert on, Samko?'

And I used to go like this:

'There'll be no concert, because that cunt Volodya nicked the balalaika.'

Meaning we're humorous and people can have a good laugh.

I always had a good laugh, too.

Then Bátori got diabetes and they had to cut his legs off. And after that he couldn't be an actor in The Hungarian Regional Theatre any more.

His name was Károly Bátori.

Alf Névéry knew lots of different languages too, but he didn't know any funny sentences, so once I told him all the funny sentences that I knew but they didn't make him laugh because he wasn't humorous. But apart from that he had lots of other good qualities, for example he was modest and didn't make a lot of noise, even though he was an artist. My sister Ivana is a great artist too, but she's an artist regarding the piano and that makes a lot of noise. And she also keeps pushing herself onto TV and onto records and it's very embarrassing that she's like that, always pushing herself everywhere and making a lot of noise.

That's why I got really worked up and I wanted to know what was what and why after Ivana told me that someone from Bratislava was going to live in the flat after Grandaddy and Uncle Otto, and that he was an artist and that he'd be renting it. But he was an artist.

Luckily, Alf Névéry was not an artist regarding the piano, he was an artist regarding writing. And luckily he didn't make writing noises, because he was a writer without being noisy. When I asked Ivana about what books he had written she told me that he had written only one book. Then she showed it to me. The book was very thin. And this is what it was called:

100 reliable of ways of committing suicide
+
99 good reasons for doing so

It was very weird.

Then Ivana told me that Alf Névéry was going to write another book, but he never wrote it because he died and it was a total disaster because they didn't want to bury him because nobody in the world, not even doctors, could work out what made him die because he had no illnesses even though he was nearly 50 years old. So they investigated him for a long time and then they wrote in the Documents that he died of failure and then he was allowed to be buried.

So he was buried at the Komárno Cemetery, even though he wasn't from Komárno, he just rented a place here.

I liked Alf Névéry because he was modest and because he called me Mr Tále because other people, even though they respect me, usually call me Samko and only my doctor calls me Mr Tále and the postwoman also calls me Mr Tále. So I was pleased that he called me Mr Tále, and I told him he could call me Samko because most people call me Samko. And after that he called me Samko even though at first he called me Mr Tále.

He said his name was Alfonz Névéry but I could just call him Alf.

So after that I called him Alf Névéry and he used to give me lots of different Karlsbad Wafers because they're the best.

He used to live in the flat next door to mine, because I have my own flat. Some people have lots of different degrees and they don't have their own flat but I have my own flat. My flat has two rooms. One room is for living and there is also another room just for having. This is where I used to live with my parents and my sisters. Grandmummy, Grandaddy and Uncle Otto used to live in a house that had to be pulled down, so they moved into a flat in the same block as us so they could be looked after because Grandmummy wasn't alive any more and Uncle Otto was disabled regarding his nerves. Then Grandaddy died and later Uncle Otto went missing and since then everyone has been waiting to see if he stops being missing, even though it's been 19 years since he first went missing.

And that's how Alf Névéry came to rent the place.

The thing is, his life of style wasn't healthy at all because he drank alcohol and smoked cigarettes and never went out into the fresh air so really he shouldn't be surprised that he died, when all he did was take baths and showers like some woman of sleazy virtue. But apart from that he was modest and he didn't make any noise.

But he wasn't humorous.

The book he wrote when he was still alive had some really weird things in it. On every page there were poems that didn't mean anything and they didn't even rhyme.

It was very weird.

That's why I thought it was OK to write a Cemetery Book that was just one page long, even though I knew that books are normally longer because I'm no retard and that's why I sent it to this man in Levice, the one who never wrote back, but I don't care if he never writes, I'm going to write another Cemetery Book, so there.

Once there was this man in Komárno and he was from Levice and his name was Zoltán Csipke and he used to rummage in rubbish bins even though he wasn't a Gypsy. Because normally it's only Gypsies that rummage in rubbish bins. But Zoltán Csipke wasn't a Gypsy and when he went out to rummage in rubbish bins he always put on white shoes and white gloves so that he wouldn't get his hands dirty. And he made a living due to this because the stuff that he found rummaging in rubbish bins he fed to his pigs and then he got very rich due to this.

And he wasn't even a Gypsy.

But then those rubbish bins made his lungs sick, so he went away to the Tatra Mountains to get a cure for his lungs, but he didn't get cured and he died.

And he used to rummage in rubbish bins even though he wasn't a Gypsy.

And everyone looked down on him because of that.

I looked down on him because of that, too.

Because even though he wasn't a Gypsy he did the sort of things that Gypsies do, like that rat-woman Angelika Édesová who steals my cardboard from the Market Place, but I'll show her if I ever catch her again stealing my cardboard from the Market Place. I'll show that rat-woman Angelika Édesová.

But the thing is, I'm not supposed to get worked up because that's very bad regarding my health so I'm not going to get worked up right?

Right.

There's just one thing I don't get, and that's why I've got to write about the Cemetery and not about lots of other nice things you can write about, like the countryside and whatever, though actually I don't go to the countryside very much because in Komárno the countryside is far away and when I come home from town I don't feel like going to the countryside because I'm very tired.

But maybe old Gusto Rúhe just makes it all up. But then again, lots of different things did happen just like he said in his fortune-telling and he also put a spell on Erik Rak. When I've finished writing this I'll write about how he put a spell on Erik Rak, because I forgot.

Old Gusto Rúhe is old and he stinks even though he was a German from Banská Štiavnica to start with. The High Ups thought he was a bad German to start with and that's why they put him in prison in Bratislava after the war. Afterwards old Gusto Rúhe said that he did time in Communist Jail but nobody believed a word he said because he's an alcoholic. And besides, he was a German and back then Germans were the baddies, and they had to go to prison because that was the law. And he used to say that he got beaten up there. And that the person that beat him most of all was called Sabopal. He always hit his toes with a hammer. But old Gusto Rúhe is an alcoholic so he must be making it up because it can't be true and he mustn't say things like that about the Communist Party. I don't want him to make up things like that. Back then making up things like that wasn't allowed, because the High Ups would have found out and it would have been be a total disaster, but now it's OK to say things like that, and I really hate that. People shouldn't be allowed to say things like that! It's not fair that people are allowed to say things now that weren't allowed before. Because now you can't tell what's what and why and how and then it's easy to get worked up, right?

Right.

Old Gusto Rúhe often urinates in the Floral Display and his lower lip hangs down almost to his chin and it's blue. It's blue like the colour blue. That's what old Gusto Rúhe's lower lip is like.

But the thing is, he doesn't have anything in the world except the Moonstone and that's why he does all his sleeping and urinating and whatever outside the Pub by the Railway Station, and only in the winter when it gets very cold he goes to spend the night in the garages at the Cemetery, because he was allowed to sleep there. But the weird thing is that when it's cold in the winter the garages get very cold too because there's no heating there. But old Gusto Rúhe goes to sleep there anyway when it gets very cold in the winter. Because he can't walk very well regarding his toes that got hammered. And the other thing old Gusto Rúhe said was that this man called Sabopal kept his hammers in a cupboard and that he had them sorted by size and each prisoner had to pick the hammer that he wanted to be beaten with from all the hammers in the cupboard.

Because that was the law.

And ever since then old Gusto Rúhe just sits and stinks in front of the Pub except when it gets cold in the winter and then he goes to sleep in the garages at the Cemetery. Because he was allowed due to his fortune-telling.

Once there was this man in Komárno whose name was Dávid Szervusz and he was the Cemetery manager. He once asked old Gusto Rúhe to tell his fortune and what Gusto Rúhe wrote on the tarmac was:

'Szervuszová mustn't take the train.'

But the thing was, this Szervusz had a mother and a wife and two daughters and all of them were called Szervuszová because they were women, so their names ended in -ová, but old Gusto Rúhe wouldn't tell him which Szervuszová mustn't take the train, so after that no Szervuszová ever took a train again. Instead, they always took the hearse wherever they went, and when Szervusz retired he bought the hearse off the Cemetery so that he could drive his family around in it, because everyone in Komárno knew that the fortune-telling had said that Szervuszová mustn't take the train. And he was scared in case anything ever happened that he would have a bad conscience about it and also that he could get into big trouble due to having allowed it when he knew about it.

Then he was killed by a stroke and he didn't have to drive the Szervuszová women in a hearse any more. His mother is 96 years old now and she's still alive and, if she doesn't take a train, she'll live until the end of her life.

When Dávid Szervusz was still alive he let old Gusto Rúhe sleep in the garages when it got very cold in winter, and when Szervusz died he was still allowed to sleep there.

That's why I sometimes think that maybe there's no law saying I have to write the Cemetery Book because maybe old Gusto Rúhe just went off his head from all the sleeping in the garages at the Cemetery. Maybe he went off his head due to that and that's why his fortune-telling got like this, right?

Right.

He only tells fortunes for men even though women would also like him to tell their fortune but he says he'll tell a woman's fortune only if she lets him grope her. In that place, you know where I mean. Between her legs. The vagina.

But women don't let him because they are indignated due to that. Only a few women did let him but even they were indignated regarding being groped, with all the people outside the Pub by the Railway Station watching.

Not even that rat-woman Angelika Édesová lets him tell her fortune because she won't let him grope her.

Even though she's a Gypsy and they don't mind being groped because they are Gypsies. Slovaks never let anyone grope them because they're not Gypsies. Once I asked old Gusto Rúhe what was up with Darinka Gunárová; then he could do the fortune-telling without any groping and all I had to do was hold the Moonstone and think of Darinka Gunárová.

Yesterday I saw Darinka Gunárová outside the Cultural Centre.

But what old Gusto Rúhe had written on the tarmac was this:

'She's got a bottomless one.'

Everybody had a good laugh and that raving queer Borka, who has several convictions on top of being a queer, said that if she had a bottomless one then 'even mine might fit in there'. That raving queer! He's got a target tattooed on his bottom and the bull's-eye is in there. You know what I mean. His rectum.

But I reported him to Karol Gunár (PhD Social Sciences), and I told him all about how he was a raving queer but Karol Gunár (PhD Social

Sciences) said that unfortunately nothing could be done about it these days because we had Democracy now.

Once I told Alf Névéry that there were people in Komárno who were queers and that there were also some women who were queers and they're called lesbians. Alf Névéry just shrugged his shoulders and I got really worked up because everyone hates queers and I thought that Alf Névéry was everyone too and would hate queers, but he just shrugged his shoulders and he wasn't even indignated. But how come there are queers when it's not allowed?

If I were a High Up I would make sure queers were not allowed and then there wouldn't be any, right?

Right.

Like Ivana, she is a great artist regarding the piano but she doesn't care regarding queers and her husband doesn't, either. Otherwise, people normally laugh at them because they think it's funny when someone's a queer.

I think it's funny, too.

And sometimes people think it's disgusting, too.

Sometimes I think it's disgusting, too.

There hasn't been a single queer or lesbian in my family because that would have been embarrassing, but luckily we were a very nice family regarding queers and lesbians. And also regarding everything else, because everyone in my family was like they should be, only Uncle Otto wasn't like he should have been because he'd been struck by lightning. The lightning went in at Uncle Otto's shoulder and it came out of his foot and lots of things happened to him due to that and he started to think that he had a Mission regarding mushrooms. And then he went missing and nobody knows if he will ever stop being missing again, because nobody knows.

Uncle Otto had a disability pension regarding his nerves due to the lightning that went in at his shoulder and came out of his foot but otherwise you couldn't tell, except that his moustache and his hair stayed black but his beard went all grey.

It was very weird.

Otherwise he was just like everyone else, except he had this Mission.

He was my Mum's brother and he was ten years older than my Mum. My Mum was ten years younger than him. My Mum had a disability pension too, but hers was not regarding nerves, hers was regarding her bad back, so they both had a disability pension. My Mum was a piano teacher regarding children but she taught at home because she had a disability pension.

My Mum's name was Emília Táleová and everyone called her Milka. My Dad's name was Emil and everyone called him Emil. My Dad was a teacher regarding woodworking and he always used to bring home all sorts of leftovers, because he said they might come in handy. My Dad was from Detva. Detva is a long way away. I've never been to Detva. My other Grandfather, his name was Emil Tále, also lived in Detva, and my Dad's brother lived in Detva too and his name was Samuel Tále. My name is Samuel Tále too but I'm not from Detva, I'm from Komárno. It's much better to be from Detva than from Komárno, because whenever I say that I'm from Komárno it makes people laugh but when I say that my Dad is from Detva they stop laughing. Because it's funny to be from Komárno but it's a serious thing to be from Detva. Detva is a long way away. I've never been there. But once I saw Detva on TV and my Dad started yelling:

'Look, look, they're showing Auntie's house in Detva!'

And he ran up to the TV to show me which house in Detva was Auntie's house but by the time he got there they were showing quite a different house which wasn't our Auntie's house in Detva.

Ivana and Margita used to go to Detva, but I've never been because Detva is a long way away.

Margita is my sister. I've got two sisters. One is called Margita and my other sister is called Ivana. Margita is five years older than me and Ivana is only one year older than me. I'm the youngest. Nobody in my family is younger than me, and that's why I'm the youngest.

Margita works at the City Hall regarding sending children to children's homes and people respect her very much due to this. She does my laundry and I have lunch at her house every Sunday. Her name is Margita Anková, because she got married. Before she got married, her name was Margita Táleová.

Before Ivana got married, her surname name was Táleová but when she got married she changed her name to Ivana Tále without -ová at the end because she is a great artist regarding the piano and when she is on records and on TV she always says that her name is Ivana Tále. Because she got married to this man whose name is Žebrák which means beggar in Czech, so it goes without saying that nobody in the world wants to be called Žebráková on records and on TV. Her husband's name is Filip Žebrák and he's an artist regarding drumming. His father was a Czech and my Dad didn't like Czechs, because he said that all Czechs are beggars, and that Slovaks are better. And besides, my Dad used to know Žebrák's Dad because they went to school together and he got offended because when they did the Tatra Eagle in class, Žebrák's Dad got the spelling wrong and he called the Tatra Eagle a Tatra Beagle. But Dad said that Žebrák was only pretending it was a mistake and he'd done it on purpose just to make fun of us Slovaks and of our culture.

My Dad didn't like Czechs or Hungarians or Russians or Jews or Communists or Gypsies or Spartakiads, or Young Pioneers, or the Socialist Youth Union, or the Union of Army Supporters, or the Revolutionary Trade Union Movement, or the Czechoslovak Hungarian Cultural Association, or the Slovak National Uprising, or the Prague Uprising, or the Women's Union, or Victorious February, or The Great October Socialist Revolution, or the Union of Czechoslovak-Soviet Friendship, or International Women's Day, or Liberation Day, and he also didn't like people calling the wartime so-called Slovak State so-called. Meaning it wasn't really independent, only so-called. My Dad always used to say that it was the Communists that were so-called. And besides he also used to listen to Radio Free Europe, and back then that was really strictly forbidden.

I told Karol Gunár (PhD Social Sciences) that my Dad listened to Radio Free Europe so that I wouldn't get into trouble for not reporting it. Karol Gunár (PhD Social Sciences) praised me very much for reporting on my Dad. But, due to him being very nice, Karol Gunár (PhD Social Sciences) forgave my father.

I loved Karol Gunár (PhD Social Sciences) because he was very nice and humorous and because he knew lots of humorous sentences, and because Darinka Gunárová was his daughter.

Yesterday I saw Darinka Gunárová outside the Cultural Centre. In the street that is a One-Way street.

Darinka Gunárová was my classmate.

Once a teacher wanted to send me to Special School but the teacher got reported and Karol Gunár (PhD Social Sciences) said I should never be sent to Special School. Because we were good friends due to me always reporting to him on everything. Because I told him that Darinka Gunárová had eaten raw green beans from the school garden and then she got sick regarding the beans, even though it wasn't allowed. He came to school to get her, and everyone said they didn't know why she was sick. But I knew, because I saw her being sick.

So after that I went to see Karol Gunár (PhD Social Sciences) and I told him I had something to report. He said I should tell him and I told him about Darinka Gunárová eating the raw green beans even though it wasn't allowed. And that this was what had made her sick.

Karol Gunár (PhD Social Sciences) then praised me very much for having told him and he said that I should always come and tell him everything. And then he said we were going to be friends from now on.

And because everybody knew that we were really good friends everybody said it should be me reciting the Young Pioneer's Oath due to being friends with Karol Gunár (PhD Social Sciences).

I said it should be me reciting it, too.

Because the Young Pioneer's Oath is the most beautiful thing in the world.

I always noticed what Darinka Gunárová was doing and when she ate raw green beans, and I always remembered everything. Because it wasn't allowed and you're not supposed do things that aren't allowed. Because that's the law.

And that is why I remembered it because I always remember everything. Even today I still remember everything and sometimes I go and report to him, even though Karol Gunár (PhD Social Sciences) isn't High Up any more, but we are still good friends and I promised I would always tell him everything. So that he knows.

Now Karol Gunár (PhD Social Sciences) isn't High Up any more. Now other people are High Up.

For example, one of the new High Ups is my sister Margita's husband. His name is Valent Anka and he is an engineer in the Docks. Because he helped to found our Independent Slovakia here in Komárno.

Margita and Ivana always argue regarding our Independence because Margita wanted it and Ivana didn't want it and she still doesn't like it even though that's not allowed, and if she keeps making me angry she'll get reported, because that's the law.

Margita loves our Independence so much that it sometimes makes her cry because she loves our Independence so much.

Our Independence would never make Ivana cry because she has no feelings. And she doesn't support our hockey players either, she supports the Czech ones. But everyone is supposed to support our hockey players.

I support our hockey players, too.

Anyway.

Once there was this man in Komárno and he was the best at founding our Independence in Komárno and his name was Dušan Janíček. And then there was this other man in Komárno whose name was Pavol Orság and he had one glass eye due to a cancer that was in there to start with and that had to be cut out along with his eye. When it got cut out, he got a glass eye instead.

So this Orság used to go around all the pubs in Komárno and spend all his money on getting drunk, and when all his money was spent on getting drunk he got poor and he had no money left to get drunk with. And that's when he started doing this disgusting thing that turned everyone's stomach.

This is the disgusting thing that Pavol Orság used to do:

If someone had an alcoholic drink in a glass, Pavol Orság would come up to them and drop his glass eye into their shot of spirits to make them disgusted and turn their stomachs, so that they wouldn't finish their shot of spirits. And then Pavol Orság would finish their alcoholic drink and have a good laugh and everyone hated him due to that.

I hated him due to that, too.

And then one day Dušan Janíček told him that he would stick a knife into his belly if he ever did it again but Pavol Orság didn't care and he dropped his glass eye into Janíček's alcoholic drink again and then Janíček pulled out a flick-knife and shoved it into Orság's belly once. Then Pavol Orság had to have an operation and after that he got better and that's why Dušan Janíček wasn't in really big trouble, because everyone in the world admitted that this thing with the eye was disgusting and stomach-turning.

After that people really respected Dušan Janíček due to sorting things out and later, when he started founding our Independence they all helped him found it because they really respected him.

Then Pavol Orság got himself frozen to death and he never made anybody's stomach turn ever again.

And this is how he got himself frozen to death: the doctors told him his cancer had got to his other eye too, so he took off all his clothes except for a blanket and he went out to freeze himself to death, because it was in the winter and it was very cold. And when they found him he was frozen dead.

Then he got himself buried at the Cemetery along with his glass eye. Sometimes when I go to the Cemetery to think up things for my Cemetery Book, I go to see all the people that are at the Cemetery because everybody is there. Grandmummy and Grandaddy are there, my Mum and Dad are there and Alf Névéry is there.

Anyway.

Tonko Szedílek is there too, and so is his Mum Katuša Szedíleková.

Tonko Szedílek was my classmate and he was my friend, but he fell off the Water Tower and broke his head and died, and then his Mum Katuša Szedíleková also died due to this disaster. They're all buried together.

There are still some wreaths on Alf Névéry's grave but I've no idea who's going to clear them away. I might even do it myself, but I don't want to be suspicious regarding clearing away wreaths from a stranger's grave instead from my own, so really it should be Ivana who should clear them away, because he was her friend regarding Bratislava and art.

Anyway, I didn't know what it would be like with Alf Névéry when Ivana told me that he was going to move in, and I was worried regarding noise because there's this man who lives on the ground floor in our block of flats whose name is Cyril Malacký and he's a writer in his spare time, but otherwise he is an attendant in the Car Park by the Church, and he wrote a book. But he wrote his book on a typing machine and that's very noisy, especially when the weather is nice and the windows are open. Then the noise it makes reaches all the way to the third floor, because that's where I live. But apart from that, Cyril Malacký is very tidy and sometimes he sweeps up the dirt round the rubbish bins. But sometimes he's noisy.

The thing is, at first I didn't know that he was being noisy regarding being a writer, all I knew was that he was an attendant at the Car Park by the Church, but I didn't know that he was a writer as well.

But then Alf Névéry told me that Cyril Malacký was a writer and that he had written a book. The book was called *Kitting Out the Idiots*. Alf Névéry also told me that in this book called *Kitting Out the Idiots* there was a person that collected waste paper in the Market Place and had a handcart with a rear-view mirror. But the thing is I have a handcart with a rear-view mirror and I collect cardboard in the Market Place, so I got very shaken aback. And I said that I would like to read this book so Alf Névéry brought it for me to read. This is what the book's title was:

Cyril Malacký

Kitting Out the Idiots

Then I started reading it but the whole first page was just one long sentence, so that relieved me because I could see that this wasn't a book for ordinary people. It had no pictures on the cover. It was very thick. The first chapter was called First Chapter. I can't think what else I could write about this book.

But the thing I don't get is why he had to write about a person with a rear-view mirror on his handcart? Why couldn't he write about a person with no rear-view mirror on the handcart? But the way he wrote it might give people all sorts of ideas, such as that Cyril Malacký lives in the same block of flats as I do, and whatever.

If it wasn't for the handcart with a rear-view mirror, people wouldn't get ideas like that.

I wouldn't get ideas like that either.

Because nobody else in Komárno has a handcart with a rear-view mirror, I'm the only one, and I have it, because without it I wouldn't be able to see what's going on behind me, and that's why Ján Boš-Mojš has to mend it for me because I am a road user just like everyone else and because that's the law.

And another important thing is that without a rear-view mirror I wouldn't be able to see who's shouting at me. Because even though people respect me for being hard-working some people still shout at me like this:

'Everybody thinks
Samko Tále stinks'

Anyway.

Except that I can see them regarding my rear-view mirror and I can shout back at them and sometimes I even get the things I shout back ready in advance so that I'm not caught off-guarded. But people almost never shout at me now because they respect me, because I'm hard-working even when the weather is bad.

Some people are not hard-working even when the weather is good.

Alf Névéry wasn't very hard-working either. Actually, he didn't work at all, because all he did was sit at home doing nothing, just looking at the picture Uncle Otto drew called *The Safe City*, and that's why I thought that it was weird that he was a writer but never wrote anything. Because you can't really be a writer without writing something, right?

Right.

For example, I am a writer because I write. Cyril Malacký is also a writer because he writes and I know that for a fact because sometimes I can hear his writing noise from the ground floor. What I don't get is how Alf Névéry was supposed to be a writer without ever writing anything.

Apart from that there aren't many writers in my family or in Komárno, even though Ivana is an artist regarding the piano and Žebrák is an artist regarding drumming. But Žebrák is not a serious artist, he's just a popular one.

Ivana and Žebrák attended lots of different schools in Bratislava regarding the piano and the drums, but the one thing I'll never get is why Ivana had to attend all those schools if she already knew how to play the piano before she went there. Because what's the point of attending a school regarding the piano if you already know how to play, right?

Right.

And she used to be very noisy regarding the piano and she never had to help with any housework such as taking out rubbish and whatever, because all she did was sit and do nothing except play the piano.

And be noisy.

Žebrák attended lots of different schools regarding drumming too and that's really weird. I don't get it why you need a school regarding drumming, because we had a drummer in our Young Pioneers and he was very good at drumming without ever attending a school regarding drumming.

Ivana has been phoning me every day for the past eighteen years to ask if I need anything, but she needn't phone me every day asking that, because I don't need anything and I can look after myself. And the other thing is that she keeps bringing me all sorts of games and clothes from her tours but I never wear the things she brings and I store them in the larder, because I have a larder, too The games are for playing in lots of different ways such as on TV, and they have names such as The War, The Red and the Black, Moulline, Little Fish and whatever. Except that I don't need any of them, because why should I, when I don't need games like that, right?

Right.

No normal person would ever wear the sorts of clothes Ivana brings back from her tours. I keep telling her not to bring me things like that from her tours, so why doesn't she stop bringing me things I don't need from her tours, right?

Right.

I keep all the things she brings me in the larder, and sometimes I give some to Margita and she sells them and gives me the money, but she can keep that money for all I care. Sometimes I tell her she should use the money to buy some alcoholic drinks regarding her husband Valent Anka.

The thing is I always have lunch at their table in their house every Sunday. And Valent Anka always says that I am his brother-in-law. But then at other times, like when he meets me in the street when I'm out and about with my handcart and he's in his car, he pretends that he can't see me. Or that he can see me but doesn't know who I am. But he can pretend as much as he likes, I don't care, because people respect me and they don't even shout at me because they respect me, so there.

And car drivers respect me, too.

Once there was this man in Komárno whose name was Feri Bezzeg, and he respected me, too He wasn't just any old driver, he was a lorry driver, and he really respected me and he always said hello to me by hooting his horn and flashing his lorry lights and I always shouted back to him like this:

'Feri Bezzeg Bros
Formula One pros.'

Except that I didn't know if Feri Bezzeg had a brother but otherwise the rhyme wouldn't rhyme.

Then he would roll down his window and throw me all sorts of sweets and chewing gum and whatever, and I would pick it up and eat it because I love sweets and chewing gum and whatever. But that's what Feri Bezzeg was like and he liked throwing sweets to other people too, because he was very kind-hearted. When we still had the Communist Party he used to drive his lorry to lots of different places and he used to bring people things they couldn't get.

And everybody loved him due to that.

I loved him due to that, too.

Once he drove his lorry to Romania because that's where he was going, and he threw sweets and chewing gum to people walking by the side of the road and then these people started fighting for the sweets and that's when Feri Bezzeg realized that they weren't normal people by the side of the road but a funeral procession by the side of the road. And he felt so sorry that this procession was so poor regarding sweets that he started throwing them whole handfuls of sweets, and the funeral procession forgot all about the funeral and started picking up the sweets and everyone got on all fours to look for the sweets. Even the most funereal ones got on all fours, including the priest and whatever, only the coffin didn't get on all fours because a coffin can't do that by itself, right?

Right.

Then Feri Bezzeg stopped throwing but the people wanted him to throw more only he had no sweets left so he stopped. But they didn't believe that he hadn't got any more, and they started banging on the lorry with their fists and Feri Bezzeg got frightened due to this and wanted to get away. But he couldn't because the people put the coffin in front of the lorry so that he wouldn't get away. Then they started smashing the windows. And then Feri Bezzeg got so scared regarding his fright that he drove right over the coffin because he didn't know what else to do. And it goes without saying that the corpse didn't care because it was dead anyway, right?

Right.

The funeral procession didn't care either and they kept looking for sweets and chewing gum and whatever.

Anyway.

After that František Bezzeg never threw any sweets out of his lorry, but people understood and they said they could understand why not.

I understood, too.

But I don't need František Bezzeg to throw me any sweets anyway because I can easily buy two hundred sweets like that if I want to.

My favourite sweets are Karlsbad Wafers even though they're not really sweets. I have to be on a sweet diet because I'm disabled regarding salty food. That is why I always have lunch at the Hospital because I'm disabled regarding salty dishes. It was Karol Gunár (PhD Social Sciences) who arranged salt-free lunches at the Hospital for me in the old days, because he is very kind.

Yesterday I saw Darinka Gunárová outside the Cultural Centre. It's not called the Cultural Centre any more because it's called Slovak National Institute now. I'd like to belong to the Slovak National Institute too because it's very nice. Margita and Valent Anka both belong to the Slovak National. Ivana and Žebrák don't belong to the Slovak National because they are different.

Darinka Gunárová was wearing golden shoes.

Honestly, I'm not making it up, she was wearing golden shoes and the shoes were not just golden but had golden shoe-laces that went up all the way, just like the kind of shoes disabled people wear. And they were all golden, all the way up to the knees.

I've never seen golden footwear like that before, not in Komárno and not on TV. Not even Ivana wears golden footwear like that, even though she's a great artist from Bratislava and wears all sorts of garments that other people would never ever wear, and even she doesn't wear golden footwear. I was so surprised regarding the golden footwear that I didn't know what was what and why and how, so I pretended that I couldn't see Darinka Gunárová even though I could.

Sometimes Ivana also wears the sort of things nobody else would wear, like on a record sleeve she wears a white tuxedo. No other woman would ever wear a tuxedo on a record sleeve or anywhere else in the world, only Ivana wears this sort of thing, and what I'd like to know is why she's always got to do the sort of thing that you're not supposed to do because people shouldn't do things they're not supposed to do, right?

Right.

Uncle Otto also used to do things that you're not supposed to do, but everyone knew that he was disabled regarding his nerves due to a bolt of lightning that went in at his shoulder and out of his foot, so everybody knew that he wasn't doing it on purpose but due to being disabled. Which was regarding his nerves. Uncle Otto was struck by lightning in a caravan in the Soviet Union during World War II, because he was a radio operator. A radio operator makes phone calls over the radio. That's what a radio operator does.

Uncle Otto was a radio operator in a caravan in Balakhashka in the Soviet Union. Balakhashka is the name of a village in the Soviet Union. He was struck while he was on the phone. When Uncle Otto recovered he realized that he had not really recovered because he could see himself lying on the ground next to the blown out caravan door and at the same time he was floating above the body that was lying there, meaning that he was floating above his own body.

Afterwards Uncle Otto told everyone how he lay there on the ground and floated above the ground at the same time but nobody believed him because Uncle Otto was disabled regarding his nerves and it said so in the Documents. And another thing that people didn't like about him was that he had a Mission and wanted to help everyone.

I didn't like him having a Mission and wanting to help everybody either.

But people wouldn't ever argue with him because they didn't want to upset him.

I never argued with him either.

But the really important thing is that nowadays all sorts of people say all sorts of things on TV about what it was like in the old days and what they had been through and sometimes it makes me think that maybe the things Uncle Otto had said about the Soviet Union really did happen. But back then nobody used to say things like that on TV and people never talked about those things either and that's why nobody believed it really happened.

I didn't believe it either.

And another thing Uncle Otto also said was that while his body was lying on the ground in Balakhashka and he was floating above it, he floated all the way to a school and it was a school regarding mushrooms. And then a teacher came in and said to Uncle Otto that from now on he would have a Mission regarding mushrooms. His mission would be to make all people brothers regarding mushrooms and to bring peace to the world.

When Uncle Otto returned to his body and home from the Soviet Union he wanted all the people all over the world to become brothers regarding using mushrooms for peace but people avoided him or laughed at him.

Only I didn't laugh at him because I hadn't been born yet.

And then he was given a disability pension.

Uncle Otto wanted to help mankind as well as all people but they did not believe him and that is why he only helped those people who were dying regarding normal doctors.

When my Mum's back hurt so badly that she couldn't sit or walk any more because all she could do was lie down or stand still due to all the pain, she could only teach children standing up, because we were very poor financially. And when the pain got really very bad she let Uncle Otto treat her, because he had wanted to treat her for a long time but she was too scared to let him treat her before.

Uncle Otto cured my Mum in one day.

But before he did it he told her that she would lose all feeling in her nose. But my Mum didn't care because she couldn't sit or walk any more due to her bad back hurting really badly so she said she didn't care if she had any feeling in her nose or not.

This is how Uncle Otto cured my Mum:

Uncle Otto took two chairs and put a ladder across them. Then he made my Mum lie on her belly on the ladder, and he tied her feet and her hands to the ladder.

It was very weird.

Then he put a stove on the floor under her head, and he put a pot on the stove. He filled the pot with water and put some Red Healers in the water. The Red Healer was a mushroom that was red all over and it was called Red Healer. It was red inside and out. It was red like the colour red.

So he put some Red Healers in the water in the pot on the stove until it started boiling and fumes started coming out and my Mum had to breathe those fumes lying there with her belly tied to the ladder. And he made her lie there tied to the ladder breathing the fumes until the next morning and until she was totally fainted and my Dad got really worked up. He got so worked up that he wanted to beat Uncle Otto up, but that didn't worry Uncle Otto at all, because he believed he had a Mission.

Then my Mum got better regarding the fainting and after that her back never ever hurt again until the day she died, but she had lost all feeling in her nose.

After that everyone in my family respected Uncle Otto very much even though he didn't care regarding being respected and kept running away from home regarding looking for mushrooms.

After my Mum lost all feeling in her nose she couldn't taste food any more and we always had to taste the food for her when she did the cooking because she kept saying that she had lost the proper nasal feeling in her nose as well as all the taste in her mouth and in her tongue. She used to say that all food tasted like old paper to her but the thing I don't get it is how my Mum knew what old paper tasted like because I never ever saw her eat old paper, and nobody else in my family ever ate old paper, because it's very bad for you.

After Uncle Otto cured my Mum's bad back my Dad said that he should try to cure me of this illness that has a proper name, because Uncle Otto had wanted to treat me for a long time but my parents wouldn't let him because they were scared. Because Uncle Otto said that he could cure me but that I would get all swollen up and black in the face to start with, and a green juice would come out of my ears and I would smell of rotten flesh. But after that I would be like my old self again and I would be like newly reborn.

My parents got very scared regarding this because they were worried that it might not work and that I might stay like that for good, all swollen and black in the face with green juice coming out of my ears and smelling of rotten flesh. So they told Uncle Otto that they'd rather I stayed as I was with this illness that has a proper name, because nobody could tell that I had it anyway because I was completely normal, just like everyone else in Komárno or anywhere in Slovakia. Right?

Right.

But Uncle Otto said it was too late now to cure me regarding this illness because I was belated for a cure, but I don't care, because I'm just like anyone else, so I don't mind having this illness that has its own name.

Because people respect me anyway because I'm hard-working. In the old days people used to shout at me like this:

'Everybody thinks
Samko Tále stinks'

And sometimes when I heard them shout like this I thought it was just as well that Uncle Otto didn't cure me because that could have made me stink for real, but now people just shout at me like that to make the rhyme rhyme, even though it's not true. But there's just one thing I don't get and that's how come it rhymes if it's not true, right?

Right.

I always report them to Karol Gunár (PhD Social Sciences) so that he knows who shouted at me and can make sure they get into trouble, and it serves them right, because they shouldn't have shouted at me. But these days people don't shout at me any more, except for that rat-woman Angelika Édesová who steals my cardboard from the Market Place. She still shouts at me sometimes but if she doesn't stop she'll see what happens to her, that Gypsy rat-woman Angelika Édesová.

There's just one thing I don't get and that's why there are so many Gypsies in Komárno, and not just in Komárno but all over the world, because what I don't get is why there have to be Gypsies in the world. I don't want there to be Gypsies in the world, they should go somewhere else, for example to Gypsyland where they came from, because ever since they came here that rat-woman Angelika Édesová has been stealing my cardboard from the Market Place. But she'll get reported because it's my cardboard. That rat-woman Angelika Édesová.

I hate Angelika Édesová.

She should be forbidden. Anyway.

Apart from me, the people in my family who hate Gypsies most are Valent Anka and Margita, because Margita's job is regarding sending children to children's homes and she says she could write a novel about the sort of things she's seen in the places where they live. But Margita has never written a novel, because she has no feeling for art.

But I do have a feeling for art and I am a writer due to that. Even though the most difficult thing about being a writer is that it makes your hand hurt. Because I write with my hand, not like some people who do their writing on a writing machine because I don't have a machine, because what do I need a machine for, this is only my second time being a writer and I don't need a machine for that, because I am very modest. And

I am also very well-off regarding money and I could easily buy 200 machines regarding writing if I wanted to. But I'm not buying any machines because I am very modest.

Anyway.

Everyone in my family has always been very modest because we were financially poor due to my Mum's disability pension and due to Ivana attending piano schools and that is why we had to be very modest so Dad used to bring all sorts of leftovers from school, for example vegetables, because he was a teacher regarding woodworking, but he also taught some classes in the school garden and that is why we often had vegetables that he brought home because we were very modest.

When we were having lunch he used to work out how much the lunch had cost us. And because the vegetables from the school garden didn't cost anything the lunch didn't cost us anything and that made everyone happy.

It made me happy, too.

Because vegetables are very good for you.

But yoghurt is best because it's really very good for you.

We always used to make our own yoghurt at home regarding being regular because it's very good for you. My Dad used to say that yoghurt was invented by the Mongols and that this went to show what a civilized people these Mongols were, because they invented yoghurt. And not just because of yoghurt, but also because they had chased the Hungarians out of Mongolia, because nobody in the world likes the Hungarians, because they are Hungarian. But everybody in the world likes Slovaks because they are Slovak.

Because Slovaks are the best people in the world and the Slovak language is the most beautiful language in the world.

That is what we were taught at school and it also said on TV that the Slovak language was the most beautiful language in the world.

And the way you can tell is because the Slovak language has the letter *Ľ*. The letter *Ľ* is the most beautiful letter in the world because it sounds really beautiful. Other languages, like the Czech language for example, can never be most beautiful in the world because they don't have the letter *Ľ*. And that's why the Slovak language is the most beautiful in the world because it has the letter *Ľ*.

The funniest language in the world is Hungarian.

And the way you can tell is because if you say something with a Hungarian accent it's very humorous and it makes everyone laugh. Because it's very funny.

It makes me laugh too because it's very funny.

The only person in the world who didn't think it was funny was Alf Névéry but he never laughed at anything in the world that was humorous because he wasn't humorous. Even though Hungarian is very humorous.

The thing is, he was very weird regarding nationalities because in his Documents it said that his nationality was Celtic.

I don't know if you're allowed to write such things in Documents because I have no idea who those Celts are and what they're doing in Slovakia so I don't know what's what and why and how. Because he always wrote it in the Documents like this: nationality — Celtic.

It was very weird.

But maybe the reason he wrote it like that was that he didn't really know what nationality, he was because nobody had told him. Because he had a very Hungarian name so maybe he just didn't want people to think that he was a Hungarian.

Ivana told me that Alf Névéry was a Slovak, but I'm no retard and I don't believe that he would have written it in Documents like this: nationality — Celtic, if he had been a Slovak. Right?

Right.

Because every Slovak is proud of being a Slovak.

I'm proud of being a Slovak, too.

But the most important thing is that Grandmummy's Grandmother was half Hungarian and her name was Eszter Csonka meaning that we weren't really the best Slovaks due to that. The very best Slovak in the world was my Grandfather from Detva because it's right in the heart of Slovakia and that's where the best Slovaks in the world come from.

Right now the best Slovak in the world in my family is my Dad's brother Samuel Tále because he lives in Detva. The next best Slovak is Valent Anka and Margita. Ivana is a very bad Slovak and she's an embarrassment for the whole family.

She's an embarrassment for me, too.

Otherwise everyone else in my family was a good Slovak, apart from Grandmummy's Grandmother who was half Hungarian and her name was Eszter Csonka.

Uncle Otto didn't turn out to be a very good Slovak either, because he wanted to help all mankind regarding mushrooms irregardlessly of nationality but the thing is, he was disabled with his nerves so he didn't have to be such a good Slovak because it wasn't the law back then.

All my friends were Slovak except that I didn't have many friends because I only had one friend and he was a Hungarian, because his Mum was Hungarian, too Her hair was so long that when she let it down it touched the bottom of her skirt.

She was very weird, not just regarding her long hair but also regarding the fact that she and Tonko were out of bedlock because she had no husband and she was single because she was not married. My other friend was Darinka Gunárová.

Yesterday I saw Darinka Gunárová outside the Cultural Centre.

She was standing on the pavement next to the One-Way Traffic Sign, and she was looking at me but I was so shaken aback that I didn't know what to do because I didn't know what was what and why and how. So I stopped because I didn't know what to do and that's when I hit the Traffic Sign with my handcart and my rear-view mirror broke off and fell to the ground. I'm usually very clever and my rear-view mirror had never broken off before because I'm very clever, so I don't get it why it had to break off this time even though I'm really clever.

It's very weird that my rear-view mirror should break off even though it never ever broke off before.

Darinka Gunárová used to be Class Prefect to start with and she had lots of white teeth. She was friends with everyone in our class including me, but I think that the only one she really wanted to be friends with was Tonko Szedílek, because that's what he was like and nearly all the girls in our class were in love with him even, though he was born out of bedlock.

But the thing is he was very tall. He was the tallest in our whole class and he was also the best regarding P.E. and that's why nearly all the girls in our class were in love with him.

I was excepted regarding P.E. so nobody could tell if I was good regarding P.E. or not, even though I'm actually very good.

But Tonko was friends with me, not with Darinka Gunárová, because he was not interested in Darinka Gunárová. He was interested in me because he always used to tell me the weirdest things in the world, like how when he turned fourteen, his Father would come and get him and how his Father would show the two of us how happy everyone was High Up There due to life being happy High Up There. And he always used to tell me that he would take me along with him when he went to climb the Water Tower.

But the thing is, he never said that Darinka Gunárová was supposed to come with us as well because he wasn't interested in her, even though I noticed that sometimes they looked at each other and I didn't know what I was supposed to think, because Tonko said that he wasn't interested in Darinka Gunárová.

And then they got reported to Karol Gunár (PhD Social Sciences) and he sorted things out. And then Tonko fell off the Water Tower and he died on the spot due to that.

I've seen lots of dead people in coffins but the only dead person I've ever seen in real life was Alf Névéry because I was the one who found him when I went to check if he'd locked up properly, because I am very careful. I am especially careful regarding things like fire and burglars and that's why, when Alf Névéry moved in next to me, I told him that I would keep a set of keys to his flat because I'm very careful and that's why I have to check and double-check lots of times that everything is locked up properly. And that is why I used to go and double-check every night that Alf Névéry had locked up properly, because if he hadn't locked up it could have been a total disaster.

Every time I have to leave my handcart I always lock it up too, because it goes without saying that if I left it unlocked someone could steal it and then I would have to go round without a handcart, but I never go around without my handcart because I'm very hard-working regarding cardboard and my handcart.

So that's why I told Alf Névéry that I was going to double-check every night if he had locked up properly because you can't be too careful. Because the other most important thing was that when I first met Alf Névéry, this is what he said to me:

'Pleased to meet you, Mr. Tále.'

It was very weird.

The thing is that even though people respect me, nobody in Komárno ever calls me Mr. Tále. Everyone calls me Samko or Samko Tále but nobody calls me Mr. Tále, because that's what they used to call my Dad and my Grandfather from Detva. So that's why I was very astonished that he called me Mr. Tále because it was very weird.

Because on TV it said that it's the most polite people who are the most dangerous, and that you can't be too careful with people like that. So I kept a set of keys, because I'm very careful.

But when I went down to double-check regarding the locking up I found the doors were unlocked, so I got very worked up and I went inside and that's when I found him sitting on a chair at the table with a blank piece of paper in front of him.

And when I found him like that I got even more worked up and I got so frightened that I got ill with my intestines, because I'm not supposed to get upset. If I'd known that Alf Névéry was planning something like this I could have got ready for it, but the way it happened I wasn't ready at all.

Plus his eyes were open as if he was looking, but you could tell that he wasn't looking and that his eyes were just open without seeing. So I went and called Ivana in Bratislava straight away because Alf Névéry was her idea in the first place. And I asked her to come and sort things out, because I was very upset and ill with my intestines.

I got really scared, although I don't normally get scared, because I thought that people might ask why he died in my flat and not in some other place, even though he hadn't been ill. Because I didn't know anything regarding any illnesses that he may have had and that's why I never thought that he could be ill. And if you don't know what's what and why and how, you might get into big trouble.

Once there was this woman in Komárno whose name was Latajnerová. She was an unmarried old maid regarding the fact that she was ugly and her breasts were no good, although she had I.Q. She used to live near the Swimming Pool and once her neighbour, whose name was Nora Honilová, asked her if she could come and look out of her balcony. Latajnerová said yes, but the thing was that Nora Honilová didn't really want to look out of her balcony, what she wanted to do was jump out regarding suicide due to this man who was in an all-Komárno dance band called The Dancing. And Nora Honilová managed to die due to her suicide jump because it was the eighth floor.

Then Latajnerová got into big trouble because people blamed her and said, what's the point of her I.Q., if she let Honilová come and look out of her balcony and that she should have known that nobody goes to see their neighbour just because they feel like looking out of their eighth-floor balcony. Latajnerová kept saying that nobody could have known what would happen, but people still blamed her for not having known and letting it happen.

But nobody blamed the man from the dance band called The Dancing because he already had one child out of bedlock and he didn't care regarding his child so nobody felt like blaming him because he wouldn't have cared about that, either.

So everyone blamed Latajnerová because she wasn't uncaring, only ugly and her breasts were no good.

After that she went to live with her mother in Nová Stráž. That's a village near Komárno. But people there blamed her too for not having known and for letting it happen.

I blamed her, too.

Her name was Anna Latajnerová.

And that's why I was frightened that people might start talking and might ask how come I allowed Alf Névéry to die in my flat without him being ill, so that's why I phoned Ivana and asked her to come, but Ivana didn't believe me on the telephone and thought that I was just making it all up, but I'm no retard, so why should I make up things like that? And besides, I could see that he wasn't moving and his eyes were open without seeing.

I didn't even touch him because I got all scared and regarding my fright I got ill with my intestines so I just waited for Ivana to come and sort things out and to make all the arrangements, because she's good at sorting things out and making all the arrangements. I could have called Margita too because she's good at making all the arrangements too, but she wouldn't have wanted to make any arrangements because she had been against renting to Alf Névéry in the first place because she had wanted the flat for her sons. But then Ivana said that Alf Névéry was going to pay 4,000 Slovak crowns per month and after that Margita agreed but she's never stopped being offended regarding the renting.

Ivana came from Bratislava really fast because she has a car, meaning that she could come really fast. Her husband Žebrák has a car, too They have one car each, meaning that they have two cars between them.

I don't have any cars even though I could easily buy 200 cars if I wanted to, because I'm economical and I'm not a squanderer, but I don't want any cars because I'm hard-working and I don't have time for a car.

Other people in Komárno have all sorts of cars too and some people even have two cars and I hate it when everyone has a car because they don't give me the right of way, even though I am a proper road user and they are obligated to give me the right of way. But they think they don't have to because all I have is a handcart.

But they are obligated and sometimes when they don't give me the right of way I write them down and they get reported. For example, at the big crossroads outside the Hospital.

The only thing I don't get is why they don't give me the right of way at the big crossroads outside the Hospital because they are obligated.

Because I have the right of way due to being a proper road user.

And then Ivana arrived and then she believed me and started to make all the arrangements and later that night I saw her cry in the toilet. Later on I will write about Ivana crying in the toilet at night.

When she'd made all the arrangements, they took him away and whatever, but they didn't want to bury him because they couldn't find a reason. Because they said that nobody dies without a reason so it had to be investigated, so they sent him to Nové Zámky because that's where they have people regarding investigating reasons. And then they said that he had died of a failure.

And this is how Ivana cried in the toilet:

I often have to go to the toilet at night for urinating purposes because my kidneys have a disability pension, so that night I also had to go for urinating purposes and that's when I found Ivana there, but she wasn't sitting on the toilet, she was sitting on the floor crying. Her head was leaning against the wall in the toilet and her mouth was totally open like she wanted to scream really badly, but no sound was coming out, she was just crying and had tears and saliva and snot streaming down her face and Ivana was shaking her head as if she wanted to wipe those things off her face onto the wall.

I got very frightened, because I'd never seen anyone cry like that, not even at a funeral or on TV or anywhere else in the world, because the way Ivana cried was really crazy.

So I went back without urinating, even though it's very bad for me.

Afterwards I often thought about Ivana crying, because it's really not a proper thing to cry like that, because Ivana is 45 years old now, because she is older than me. Ivana cried as if she was little and that's not a proper thing to do if you're 45 years old and have three children and if you're on TV all the time, so it isn't proper at all.

But if Ivana ever gets nasty with me regarding dressing and washing myself, I will report her to Žebrák about her crying when Alf Névéry died. Because I hate Ivana when she comes to my flat and goes round sniffing as if I stank, and I hate her always bringing me new clothes and saying that I'm not hygienical. Alf Névéry was hygienical and it didn't do him any good, because he did not lead a healthy life of style because he drank alcohol, smoked cigarettes and never drank yoghurt, even though it's very good for you regarding health. Anyway.

And maybe that's why the doctors couldn't find a reason because they didn't know him and they didn't know that he used to leave the lights on all night and that he slept during the day because he was the wrong way round. If they'd asked me I'd have told them about him being the wrong way round, but doctors get very upset if you try to tell them what to do so I'm not telling them what to do regarding the reason and they can figure it out for themselves, right?

Right.

Once I asked old Gusto Rúhe why Alf Névéry had died, and this is what he wrote on the tarmac after doing all his burping and slurping:

'Because.'

That made me very angry and upset, because fortune-telling is supposed to be about telling people's fortunes so I started swearing at him because first he'd made me buy him a shot of spirits, and then he wrote this rubbish but he gave me a look and I got frightened that he might put a spell on me like he did on Erik Rak so I stopped swearing because old Gusto Rúhe can write any old rubbish for all I care, right?

Right.

Later I will write about him putting a spell on Erik Rak because I keep forgetting to.

The thing is that people were scared of him after he put a spell on Erik Rak and nobody was willing to do anything about him and make sure he would get into big trouble. Not even Karol Gunár (PhD Social Sciences) was willing to do anything about him and to make sure that he'd get into big trouble, even though he is very kind and not scared of anything in the world.

Yesterday I saw Darinka Gunárová outside the Cultural Centre. I pretended not to see her due to the golden shoes and all the rest of it, but Darinka Gunárová saw me and she called out to me.

She called out my name like this:

'Samko!'

And then she waved at me.

So I pretended that I only noticed her just then, even though I had noticed her as soon as I saw her.

I always notice everything, for example when my Dad and Margita and Ivana went to Detva to visit my Grandfather, my Mum and I used to look at picture books and my Mum asked me to notice things, for example how many bunnies there were in a picture. And I always noticed all the bunnies and even my Mum was surprised how I noticed all the bunnies.

Anyway.

And when my Dad and Margita and Ivana came back from Detva and started talking about the things that had happened in Detva, my Mum always told them that I had noticed all the bunnies in the book.

And I always got praised for it.

I always notice all the people on the pavement too, including the people that cross over to the other side of the road when they notice me and then I call out their names extra loud so that they don't think that I didn't notice them.

And I always used to notice all the bunnies, too.

If I ever notice that rat-woman Angelika Édesová again stealing my cardboard from the Market Place, I will show her, that rat-woman Angelika Édesová. Because I told the shopkeepers in the Market Place that all the cardboard in the Market is mine, so it's mine. Because I said so. If other people said it was theirs it would be theirs. But I said it first so it's mine, right?

Right.

Once there was this man in Komárno who used to keep his cardboard for me because I had asked him to and because he was kind-hearted, and he never gave his cardboard to anyone else and he kept it just for me because he was very kind-hearted and his name was Adam Miller.

Adam Miller was a very modest shopkeeper because he had three daughters as well as a mother and a wife and a sister. They all lived in the same flat and that's why they had to be very modest. But Adam Miller was also very modest because he was kind-hearted and he used to keep cardboard for me due to his kind-heartedness.

But then he got a very serious illness which was so serious he couldn't be a shopkeeper any more and had to stay at home all the time. And due to that he started to prepare his last wish. A last wish is the kind of wish that people make regarding their last wish.

And when Adam Miller died it turned out that he had come up with a last wish that outraged everyone and it made all the Miller women cry because Miller's last wish was to be buried with his trousers undone so that it would stick out from his trousers. That thing. His penis.

And his other last wish was that they should cover both his eyes with a black patch so that he would never have to look at this bunch of dogs again. But what he really meant was not dogs, but humans. And all the Miller women cried regarding this outrage because it was very offensive but the thing was, it was Miller's last wish which meant that they had to do it. So they didn't know what was what and why and how and everyone felt sorry for them and everyone was outraged.

I was outraged, too.

Because if they had followed Miller's last wish it would have offended the whole Cemetery, and the whole Cemetery would have been outraged.

So in the end the Miller women said that Adam Miller had been so ill that he didn't know what he was doing, which meant that his last wish didn't really count. And that relieved everyone.

It relieved me, too.

So then they could bury Adam Miller properly and after that everyone remembered him fondly, and everyone said what a modest shopkeeper and what a kind-hearted man he had been.

I remembered him fondly, too.

Adam Miller was a shopkeeper regarding women's clothing.

Anyway.

Once Alf Névéry heard me swear at people who were shouting at me and he said that I swore like Miller. That gave me a real fright because I didn't know which Miller he meant, because Adam Miller was a very kind-hearted man and everyone remembered him very fondly. But he said that he meant a totally different Miller who wasn't from Komárno but from America and that he wasn't swearing in real life, only in books. That relieved me. And I said that I would like to see this Miller from America swearing, but Alf Névéry said that he didn't have his book in Slovak, only in English. So I have never found out how this Miller from America swore. Because America is a long way away.

Anyway.

But one thing I don't get is this. If Alf Névéry knew so many different languages from all around the world, how come he never laughed at the humorous sentences that are humorous in all the different languages?

I'm sure Alf Névéry would have laughed if he had been humorous. But he wasn't humorous and that's why he never laughed.

For example, I am very humorous. The way you can tell that I'm humorous is regarding the jokes I can tell. One of the jokes I can tell goes like this:

Two men are talking, and the first man says to the second, 'My dog's got no nose.' The other man asks him, 'How does he smell?' The first man answers, 'Awful!'

Meaning smells things, and smells like stinks. The first time 'smell' means 'sniffing', the second time 'stinking'. It's a very good joke because you have to have I.Q. to get the thing about smelling.

But I've got I.Q. and I'm very humorous, too.

But what I hate is when people tell jokes about the Communists. Nobody used to tell more jokes about the Communists than my Dad. Except that he used to tell jokes about others, too Like the Jews, the Partisans, the Hungarians and the Russians.

This joke about the dog smelling, I told it to Žebrák too because it's a joke that I always tell everyone, and Žebrák had a good laugh but not due to the joke but because he likes to make up all sorts of funny rhymes. They don't have any real meaning, they are just rhymes that rhyme. For example, he makes up rhymes that go like this:

Slap her / Slapper

or

Master Bait / Masturbate

or

Polygon / Polly gone

Anyway.

Rhymes like this can be quite funny and sometimes they make me laugh but they are not half as funny as the sentence:

Attention, attention, the balalaika concert is off because that cunt Volodya nicked the balalaika.

That's the funniest humorous sentence ever. It makes me laugh every time I say it.

My Grandfather from Detva also knew lots of funny and humorous sentences. For example the one that goes like this:

'*Kezét csókolom*, how d'you do?
That's in Hungarian, so sod you!'

Anyway.

Because every time my Grandfather from Detva came to visit us he used to ask if I used the Hungarian greeting *kezét csókolom*. My Grandfather from Detva always came to visit us along with my Dad's older brother. They always went everywhere together, because he never got married because he survived a disaster.

And when they came to visit us they used to sit in the kitchen with my Dad and drink alcohol that they brought from Detva, and they used to ask why there were so many Hungarians in Komárno. And they kept saying that someone should shoot them all so there wouldn't be so many of them around. But how am I supposed to know why there are so many Hungarians around if nobody's ever told me?

When I've finished writing this I will write about the disaster my Dad's older brother survived.

They used to visit us when they wanted Grandmummy to make them a new suit, because she always had to make clothes for the whole family due to being a tailor.

Once my Grandfather from Detva came to visit us along with my Dad's older brother and they brought alcoholic drink and my Grandfather from Detva said that I should have a drink with them. But I said I couldn't have a drink with them because I wasn't allowed to drink alcoholic drinks, but my Grandfather from Detva said that it wasn't nice of me to use Hungarian greetings such as *kezét csókolom* but refuse to have a drink with them. Then he got a cup out of the cupboard and poured me an alcoholic drink, so I drank it. He got the first cup in the cupboard but it happened to be the one we used for keeping leftover candles, because my Dad used to say that those leftovers might come in handy one day, so I ended up drinking an alcoholic drink along with the leftovers and I had to throw up straight away because it was disgusting. That's when my Dad came in and wondered why I'd thrown up in the kitchen, so I told him so that he would know. My Dad got so cross that he threw out his elder brother along with my Grandfather from Detva.

He needed an hour to calm down and when he was calm again he asked my Mum to find them and say sorry and please come back. So my Mum went and found them, and they came back and they stayed in the kitchen drinking alcohol until the next morning and until they all made up and loved each other and never argued again. And my Dad was so ill the next morning that my Mum had to phone the school and tell them that Dad couldn't come to work due to being sick.

When Grandmummy was still alive they used visit us regularly because they needed new suits. But when Grandmummy died they stopped visiting us because Detva is a long way away.

And now I shall write about the disaster that my Dad's older brother survived. The disaster that my Dad's older brother survived happened like this:

When he was a young man my Dad's older brother wanted to get married and he found a woman he wanted to marry who was also from Detva. They were going to get married and everything was ready for the wedding which was supposed to be on a Saturday. And then on the Tuesday before the wedding the woman who was supposed to marry my

Dad's older brother and be his wife went out gathering mushrooms and she gathered enough mushrooms for the whole family, because there are lots of mushrooms in Detva.

My Dad's mother cooked the mushrooms and invited everyone including the woman who was going to marry my Dad's older brother and be his wife. And because my Dad's mother was humorous she said that if the mushrooms were poisonous, they might as well all kick the bucket together and so they all had some mushrooms. Except for my Grandfather from Detva because he was away from Detva when it happened. And the next day my Grandmother from Detva died and so did the woman who was going to marry my Dad's older brother and be his wife; and my Dad's older brother very nearly died too except that he didn't. He stayed in hospital for three weeks and then he came home because he got better, except that his face stayed purple for the rest of his life.

His face was purple like the colour purple.

He never got married after that and everyone felt very sorry for him regarding the great disaster he had survived.

But the main thing was that it was meant to be a Saturday wedding but instead it was a Saturday funeral and everyone said how very moving it was that there was a funeral instead of a wedding and everyone was very moved.

After that everyone said that it was the most beautiful funeral because there were two coffins together and my Dad's older brother had very nearly died, too Except that he didn't, and he got better apart from his face that has never lost the purple colour, and people were sometimes scared of him due to this because they didn't know that he was like that due to poisonous mushrooms.

But luckily he used to wear a welder's hat and that way people couldn't see that his face was purple. The reason why he wore a welder's hat was because he was a welding instructor because there is a big demand for welders in Detva.

Every time he came to visit he told us funny stories regarding welding, for example the things that people said during welding exams. Because you can't become a welder just like that, first you have to get certified regarding an exam. Because it's not easy to be a welder.

He knew lots of funny stories about welding exams and some of them were so funny that he told them maybe twenty times. For example the one about this man who said this during his exam:

'If a welder lets it slip out without protection he will have to bear the consequences for the rest of his life.'

That was very humorous.

Meaning he would bear the consequences for the rest of his life if he let it slip out without protection.

Anyway.

But the best thing was that people thought his face was so purple due to welding. But apart from that he was very popular due to his funny stories.

He was very popular with everyone in my family too, except that there was a big problem with Uncle Otto, because he had a Mission regarding mushrooms and my Dad's older brother hated mushrooms which goes without saying. So they always had to keep them separated to stop them arguing, because they always argued whenever they met if nobody separated them.

So every time we expected visitors from Detva, they used to lock Uncle Otto in Grandmummy's and Grandaddy's flat in the back room, the one they used as store-room because they didn't have a larder even though they had a two-bedroom flat. But they had no larder. Because that was in the part of town where they later built this big chimney and all the houses there had to be torn down to make room for the big chimney.

In those days Grandmummy and Grandaddy and Uncle Otto used to live all together because he was their son and he had to be looked after regarding everything.

The back room in their house had a black table made of marble and they used it for storing vegetables and eggs and whatever, because in those days you couldn't get a refrigerator just like that.

This table used to frighten me because Grandmummy once told me that there was blood on that table and I didn't know what was what and why and how and I was really scared of it because it was black and had a marble top. Only it didn't have any chairs.

And every time they locked Uncle Otto in the larder to keep him separated, they would bring in an armchair to make him comfortable.

And after the visitors left they would let him out again.

Otherwise there were never any problems with Uncle Otto because otherwise he was very popular.

Once I asked Grandaddy why there was blood on the marble table and Grandaddy got very upset and cross and said that we would all get into big trouble if Grandmummy kept saying things like that. But the thing was, Grandmummy used to smoke cigarettes and read detective stories and do things that nobody else's grandmother used to do, and that's why I didn't know what was what and why and how, so I wanted to know what it was about the blood, but Grandaddy wouldn't tell me, and all he would say was that Grandmummy was going to get us all into big trouble. But I wanted to know what it was about the blood anyway so I asked Grandmummy, and she told me that our black table made of marble as well as our piano had came from an auction where you could buy things left behind by the Jews.

Because a long time ago, when the Jews went away, for example to concentration camps, they had to leave their things behind and the things had to be sold, because why would Jews need things like a piano in a concentration camp, right?

Right.

Grandmummy swore that she would never sit at the table with the marble top and that's why Grandaddy had to keep it in the back room regarding keeping vegetables fresh and also because we didn't have any chairs to go with it anyway.

Grandmummy didn't need to sit at the piano even though it did have a chair because she didn't know how to play.

The piano was black too but it wasn't made of marble, it was made of wood and its name was Petroff-Grand. It lived in the main room and its feet sat in little ashtrays to stop them from leaving marks on the carpet even though we had no carpet.

I wanted to ask my Mum if there was blood on the piano too, but I didn't because I didn't want to know about the blood on the piano even though I knew that it wasn't real blood, because I'm no retard and I know that the blood wasn't real, only regarding the Jews. So it wasn't real blood.

Once there was this man in Komárno who was a Jew. His name was Goldstein and I used to shout at him like this:

'Bertík Goldstein
Lost his foreskin.'

Because his name was Bertík Goldstein and it rhymed with the rhyme and that's why it was very humorous. It always made me laugh a lot.

It made other people laugh, too.

Later on he left to emigrate to Israel but he died as soon as he got to the airport because he was so happy to be in Israel that he died of joy at the airport.

When he was still living in Komárno he used to mend bicycles and I used to shout at him like this: 'Bertík Goldstein lost his foreskin', even though I didn't know if he had a bit of his skin cut off down there or not, but that's what people say about the Jews because it is very humorous.

There's just one thing I don't get and that's why the Jews have a bit of their skin cut off down there. You know where I mean. On their penis. Because then everyone can tell that they are Jews straight away and they get sent straight to concentration camps and whatever, because as soon as they take off their underpants they can't pretend that they're not Jews because it is obvious they're Jews. Right?

Right.

And another thing I don't get is how they could tell with women. Maybe they made them take some tests and it showed up in the tests.

I often have to go for all sorts of tests, especially due to my disability regarding urine. So that I can have all sorts of tests done on my urine.

Nowadays people don't find urine funny any more, but when I was at school and we had to take a urine sample to the school doctor for a check-up, all the children thought it was very funny. But that's not allowed, and a proper Young Pioneer doesn't find urine funny because he is good.

And if anyone finds it funny he'll get reported and he'll get into big trouble.

A good Young Pioneer has lots of good qualities, like not finding urine funny, and like collecting waste paper. Anyway.

I've been collecting waste paper ever since I was little and I have always collected lots and lots of it. I collected so much waste paper that I came top in the whole school and that's when I got given the book called *The Young Pioneer's Heart* and I got reported on the school radio.

In the old days you didn't get to come top just like that, because there wasn't much cardboard around then, there was just waste paper which is much lighter, so a Young Pioneer had to make a real effort to come top and of the whole school at that.

But I always came top.

Sometimes I shared some of my waste paper with Darinka Gunárová so that she would also get praised, because I always had lots of waste paper due to being hard-working.

Yesterday I saw Darinka Gunárová outside the Cultural Centre.

The golden shoes she was wearing had really high heels and they made Darinka Gunárová very tall. They made her much taller than me even though she used to be only normally taller than me. Because she never used to be that tall, like my sister Ivana for example. Ivana is so tall that she has to bring her own piano stool when she has a concert, that's how tall she is.

The only thing I don't get is why someone who's as tall as Ivana could cry so much in the toilet after Alf Névéry died, because he wasn't really all that tall, he was just normal, meaning he wasn't as tall as Ivana. And that's why it's out of the question that Ivana could do such a thing because she was much taller than Alf Névéry.

Because that's out of the question.

She got her tallness from our Grandfather from Detva who was so tall that he had to take his hat off to get through the door. My Dad's older brother was also tall but not quite so tall. My Dad was the least tall of them all.

My Grandfather from Detva used to say that the taller you are, the better a Slovak you are.

But that can't be true because I'm a very good Slovak even though I'm only 152 centimetres tall, but that's not due to my nationality, it's just due to this illness of mine that has a proper name.

And Ivana isn't a good Slovak, even though she is very tall. Meaning it's got nothing to do with nationality at all.

That's just is how it is.

And that's why I hate it when people say things that aren't true because then people might think it's true when isn't really true.

I'm a really good Slovak and I used to be a really good Young Pioneer, too But the one thing I don't get is why it had to be me who got a Young Pioneer's Scarf that wasn't properly red but sort of orange. That's why sometimes I thought that people might wonder why my scarf wasn't properly red like all proper Young Pioneers' Scarves and that they might think that I was different. But I'm not different, I'm just like everyone else in the world and the only reason I have a disability pension is because of my kidneys and not because of this illness that has a proper name and makes you stop growing and stops your beard from growing.

So there.

Alf Névéry once told me that German Democratic Pioneers had Pioneer Scarves that were just like mine and he promised to show me a picture but he never did because he died, and when Ivana was packing up his things because he'd been divorced regarding his wife, so there wasn't anyone else to pack up his things, I asked her to find me the picture of the German Democratic Pioneers but she went crazy and wouldn't even talk to me and wouldn't let me anywhere near his things as if I was going to rummage in them. But I wasn't going to rummage, I just wanted her to find me that picture.

Then Ivana told me to take all of Alf Névéry's things that were left over to Recycling but I didn't because I didn't want to get into trouble with that idiot Krkan regarding things that weren't mine. I don't see why Ivana can't take it to Recycling herself. Because I know that idiot Krkan would ask all sorts of questions and I don't have time for silly things like talking to that idiot Krkan who takes it from Angelika Édesová when it's wet, but won't take it from me. I could go to another place for Recycling if I wanted to, because everyone knows me and everyone respects me.

But I don't really like to go to other places for Recycling because this one is close by and it's really handy because it's close by. I only wish that idiot Krkan didn't work there.

He hasn't got any good qualities at all.

The only thing I don't get is why the High Ups don't send him away.

I have asked Karol Gunár (PhD Social Sciences) lots of times to get the High Ups to send him away, but he just said that we got what we wanted, so we had Democracy now. But it's not what I wanted and anyway, nobody asked me if that's what I wanted, so I don't get it. Why can't Karol Gunár (PhD Social Sciences) sort out that idiot Krkan and have him sent away? Because this isn't what I wanted.

Once, when this woman teacher wanted to send me to Special School, he sorted it all out and I didn't get sent there. Grandaddy went to see him and told him that the teacher wanted to send me to Special School but that I didn't want to go because it was a school for retards and I was no retard, and besides, I was friends with Karol Gunár (PhD Social Sciences).

Grandaddy didn't want me to go to Special School either, because he was in the Communist Party and it would have been an embarrassment for him if I went to Special School that was just for retards.

Grandaddy was in the Local Party Cell which was for people who wanted to belong to the Communist Party even after they retired. Grandaddy had a special Notebook regarding the Local Cell, and he used to write down all sorts of things in his Notebook, which was so important that I wasn't even allowed to look inside. That's how important his Notebook was, even though it didn't have lined pages.

And that's why he could go and see Karol Gunár (PhD Social Sciences) because he was sort of my classmate regarding Darinka Gunárová, and he could ask him to make sure that I wasn't sent away and that's why I was never sent away because he was my friend and he sorted it all out.

Yesterday I saw Darinka Gunárová outside the Cultural Centre. And she called out to me and waved to me, and then she crossed the road to where I was standing. I couldn't cross the road because I had my handcart so I couldn't cross the road just like that. So she crossed the road herself. And this is what she said to me:

'Is it you Samko?'

Meaning, if it was me. But I didn't know what to say because it goes without saying that it was me, because there's nobody else in Komárno like me, so obviously it had to be me. And that's why I didn't know what to say.

But there are other people in Komárno who collect cardboard, like that rat-woman Angelika Édesová, or this Czech man and his wife whose name is Nepil which means 'Didn't Drink'. Usually I shout at him like this:

'Nepil was a rotter
Didn't drink no water.'

Meaning he didn't drink any water. That's very humorous, right?
Right.

His name is Vladimír Nepil and his wife's name is Kordula Nepilová.

I'm not even sure if a name like that even exists because I've never met anyone else with a name like that, not even on TV. But that's what Nepilová is called. Kordula.

It's very weird.

But otherwise they are very nice people and they never steal my cardboard from the Market Place, even though they are Czechs. But I wonder about the name Kordula anyway, because I'm not sure they haven't just made it up. Because names like that don't exist any more.

And the other good thing about them is that they don't go around speaking Czech. They speak Slovak, and everybody likes that. And they're not trying to push other people around due to being Czech and they always speak Slovak. Hungarians are always trying to push other people around due to being Hungarians and they always speak Hungarian.

Nobody likes that.

I don't like it either.

They should speak Slovak, and if they don't they will get reported.

My grandmother Grandmummy spoke Slovak too even though her mother was half Hungarian and her name was Eszter Csonka. But that's what Grandmummy was like, and she also used to smoke cigarettes and read Allan Wilton, which wasn't allowed even wrapped up. And that's why nobody took her seriously because there was some of that Hungarian blood in her. Although you couldn't tell that she had any Hungarian blood just by looking at her.

You really couldn't tell by looking. Not even a little bit.

So this Nepil was a Czech, and when he was younger he used to do gymnastics on a horse and he even won a medal. People always asked him if his things didn't get squashed when he exercised on the horse. But they didn't mean a real horse, what they meant was an exercise horse. The kind that's used in gymnastics and on TV, too And Nepil always said that his things got squashed so many times that they turned blue like the blue wedge on the Czechoslovak national flag. And everybody was happy to hear that they turned blue. Those things down there, you know what I mean.

Our new Slovak national flag doesn't have a blue wedge and that makes everyone very happy, too.

It makes me very happy, too.

And then there's this other man in Komárno who collects cardboard whose name is Vojtech Inas and he's a Gypsy. But the most important about Vojtech Inas is that he wears glasses. I've never met any other Gypsy who wears glasses, and I think people should watch Vojtech Inas regarding that, because a Gypsy who wears glasses could be very dangerous because he could pretend to have I.Q.

And that's why when I see him I always keep an eye on him to make sure he doesn't steal anything from my handcart because he wears glasses and that's really very weird.

I don't wear glasses myself.

My eyesight is very good and that's why I always notice everything.

Apart from me, there are all sorts of other people in Komárno who make deliveries, but they only do it from time to time. But I've been making deliveries for twenty-eight years. And that rat-woman Angelika Édesová had better stop stealing my cardboard, or I'll show her.

But the thing is, I'm not supposed to get worked up.

Now that my handcart is in Ján Boš-Mojš's workshop I don't need to get worked up about people stealing my cardboard from the Market Place because I don't care who steals it. Because without my rear-view mirror I can't collect it anyway, because I can't see what's behind me, which means that I can't see who's shouting at me either.

And that's why it's out of the question.

My rear-view mirror has never broken off before. This is the first time it happened and I had to take it to Ján Boš-Mojš's workshop to get it

welded back because you need special tools to do that. You can't just do it
like that.

And while I'm waiting for it to get welded back on, I can be a writer,
because once it gets fixed I won't have time for silly things like that. And
then I won't be able to write the Cemetery Book.

But the thing I don't get is why it's got to be about the Cemetery.
Maybe it's not really the law because old Gusto Rúhe is very old and he's
an alcoholic, because he lives on alcohol, so maybe he is just pretending
regarding the Moonstone to make people buy him shots of alcohol.

And then he also wrote the word Boy on the tarmac. What I would
really like to know why he had to add that word. Because I'm not a boy,
I'll be forty-four years old soon, so I'd like to know what old Gusto Rúhe
meant by writing the word Boy? What he should have written is Man,
right?

Right.

Grandaddy used to call me Boy, too He used to say, if we don't get
the Boy sorted out it will be a disaster, and then he used to go and see
Karol Gunár (PhD Social Sciences) and ask him to sort things out. And
when they met in the street, Grandaddy would greet him like this:

'Proletarian greetings, Comrade!'

And then he would raise his hat and greet the wife of Karol Gunár
(PhD Social Sciences) like this:

'Proletarian greetings to Madame Comrade, too'

I used to love it when people said 'Proletarian greetings'. I wish
people would still say that, but nobody says it any more because now it's
not allowed. And if people said it they would get into big trouble.

But whenever my Dad heard this greeting he always said this thing
about the secret police. What he used to say was this:

'Proletarian greetings,
Secret police beatings!'

But it's really bad to say things like that about the secret police and
beatings and whatever. People who say things like that will get reported
on and they will be in big trouble.

When my Dad said things like that I was always really scared that the
High Ups might find out and they might ask me why I hadn't reported my
Dad for saying things like that about them.

That's why I was happier being with Grandaddy because he never said things like that, and also because he had a Notebook regarding the Local Party Cell which was a very important Notebook.

He used to greet people by saying 'Proletarian greetings!' and he used to subscribe to *Party Life*.

Party Life was a newspaper that nobody used to read, but Grandaddy was scared to cancel it because he said the High Ups were keeping an eye on it and anyone who cancelled would get into big trouble. That's why he never cancelled.

Grandmummy used *Party Life* to wrap up Allan Wilton and to fire up the stove, because they had a stove. Because in the old days you couldn't have central heating just like that. Nowadays, anyone can have central heating just like that.

My grandparents had two stoves because they had two rooms, except that the third one wasn't a room. It was the larder which had the table with the marble top where Uncle Otto grew his mushrooms. They didn't need a stove there, because mushrooms don't like heat. What mushrooms like is humidity. And that's why sometimes the room really stank from time to time because some of the mushrooms that Uncle Otto grew were very smelly.

The *Party Life* newspaper always had a humorous cartoon on the last page. Usually the cartoons were about Americans. They were very serious and very instructive. Like, for example, this cartoon that showed an American soldier who had put a bomb inside some tinned food and gave the tin to a little black girl saying:

'Here you are, have some of our food aid.'

Meaning it was their food aid.

And the way you could tell that he was an American soldier was due to the writing on his hat. It was very instructive as well as very humorous.

But mainly it was very instructive.

Karol Gunár (PhD Social Sciences) was also very humorous as well as very modest, and the way you could tell was that when he clinked glasses he always used to say:

'Proletarians of the world, imbibe!'

That was humorous and everyone could see that Karol Gunár (PhD Social Sciences) was very modest and that he wasn't stuck up at all, even though he was High Up. And then everyone had a good laugh, because it was very humorous.

As well as very modest.

In addition to that, he used to wear a black fur hat that he called a Persian, just like the one the First Working Class President Klement Gottwald used to wear. And he used to say that he was going to be the Second Working Class President because they wore the same kind of hat and had the same initial letters. You get initial letters when a name starts with a first letter.

My initial letters are S.T.

Karol Gunár's (PhD Social Sciences) initial letters were K.G. Just like Klement Gottwald's.

Darinka Gunárová's initial letters were D.G. Later they became D.M. And now they are D.Q.

I've got her in my Surnames Notebook under all these initial letters. But in my Christian Names Notebook I've got her down only under *D*.

Yesterday I saw Darinka Gunárová outside the Cultural Centre. She was wearing a skirt that was so short that there was room for another skirt. The skirt she was wearing was black. It was very short. That's what the skirt Darinka Gunárová was wearing was like.

Once there was this woman in Komárno whose name was Veronika Osladičová and she used to wear skirts that were so short that every time she bent over it was a total disaster. But the reason she wore skirts like that was because she wanted to be a provocation, because she was that sort of woman. You know what I mean. A woman of sleazy virtue. She used to ride a bicycle and offer to do sexual things with men for money.

She offered that to me, too.

Once I met her by the Statue of the Sailor, and this is what she said: 'Would you like me to warm you up, Samko?'

But I told her all the swearing words that I could think of. How dare that woman Veronika Osladičová say things like that to me? I'm no retard and I knew what she was up to. What she was up to was doing sexual things for money, but how dare she say things like that to me, like offering to warm me up? I don't need anyone to warm me up, because I've got a proper padded coat and I wear thermal underwear as well as padded shoes.

So I kept swearing at her until she went away.

Later this Greek man came to live in Komárno and he fell in love with Veronika Osladičová because he was the son of Greek communist fighters and he was going to marry her because he didn't know about her.

His name was Michalis Demetropullossis.

People didn't know what to do about him not knowing and wanting to marry her because he didn't know that people despised her. Especially women. So people decided to tell him, to make sure that he saw the light.

At first Michalis Demetropullossis didn't believe them and wanted to beat them up but then people said he should look at the kinds of skirts she wore, and what a total disaster it was when she bent over. And then Michalis Demetropullossis had to admit they were right and he got very unhappy and moved away from Komárno.

Veronika Osladičová was unhappy too, but she didn't move away.

So there was a happy ending and people were pleased that they had made him see the light and that it all turned out right in the end.

I was pleased, too.

Anyway.

That's why I was really surprised to see Darinka Gunárová wearing the same kind of skirt, and I didn't know what was what and why and how.

I don't normally get surprised very often because I usually know what's what and why and how and when I say that something will happen then things almost always turn out that way. For example, when I say:

'You'll see.'

Then things often turn out exactly like I said.

Like with that nasty Borka, the raving queer. Once he tried to put his arm round my shoulder but I wouldn't let him because he's got a bull's-eye tattooed around that place down there, you know what I mean, so I told him that he would end up in jail, and he did, because I told him so.

Afterwards I told everyone that I had told him so and that I always knew that nasty Borka would end up in jail.

Margita is another one who knows in advance how things will turn out and when they do, she always says:

'You see, I told you so and how right I was!'

She is almost always right regarding having told us so, for example she said that Ivana shouldn't rent to Alf Névéry because it wasn't going to end well. And she said that Czechoslovakia would be over soon, because otherwise things wouldn't end well. And afterwards she said she had told us so and how right she was.

Margita is very proud of having told us so.

Old Gusto Rúhe also says things in advance, but he doesn't care if they turn out the way he said, because he doesn't even remember what he said a minute ago, because he's old and he's an alcoholic and his lower lip hangs down to his chin and he's disgusting due to that.

Once I went to see him regarding his fortune-telling that said 'Will write the Cemetery Book. Boy,' because I wanted to know what he meant by it but he refused to tell my fortune again and said he had already told my fortune once, even though he couldn't remember what it was. So I told him what his fortune-telling was regarding my fortune and old Gusto Rúhe just laughed and said, oh well, in that case it must be true, and asked me to get him another shot of spirits or a beer, so I got him a beer because that's cheaper.

Everyone in Komárno always gets him alcoholic drinks, because nobody wants to have a spell put on them like Erik Rak, which goes without saying.

When I'm done writing this I will write about how he put a spell on Erik Rak.

I never asked him again, because I knew I would just end up buying him another alcoholic drink and he wouldn't tell me anyway why I'm supposed to write about the Cemetery, because that's what he's like.

Old Gusto Rúhe wasn't like that to start with. To start with, he used to be totally different, meaning that he was totally normal, but he got to be like that due to being beaten in jail with hammers, and he had to pick the one to be beaten with.

Once he got such a bad beating with a hammer on his toes and on his head that he fainted, and while he was fainted he had a dream that went like this:

He dreamt that he was in a waiting room with lots of people and one of them came up to him and said that his name was Ladislav Hrobárik and that he was Tax Office Director in Bánovce nad Bebravou and that his train was due to arrive soon. Old Gusto Rúhe said that his name was Augustín Rúhe and that he used to be a student but couldn't finish his studies. Then they shook hands.

Then Ladislav Hrobárik said that he wanted to ask him for help and old Gusto Rúhe agreed to help him. Ladislav Hrobárik told him to go and find his wife Elena Hrobáriková in Bánovce nad Bebravou and tell her that he had buried something in the garden, exactly half-way between the wall of their house and the well. He said they should dig up the garden and old Gusto Rúhe could keep whatever they found there, except for a stone that was yellow and transparent and was called Moonstone. His wife Elena Hrobáriková should keep the stone because it was a stone regarding making all wishes come true.

And he said that she knew what wish to make.

Old Gusto Rúhe promised he would do that.

Then Ladislav Hrobárik left because his train arrived.

When old Gusto Rúhe came out of his fainting fit he was very surprised not to be in a waiting room but in jail in Bratislava, and that's where he stayed for another four years and nine months. And while he was there, he found out that a man named Ladislav Hrobárik, who used to be Tax Office Director in Bánovce nad Bebravou and later was in charge of the auctions regarding Jews and their property, had been in the same jail in Bratislava.

And later he found out that Ladislav Hrobárik had died due to the hammers he had to pick regarding the beating.

After that old Gusto Rúhe was released from jail in Bratislava because it turned out he that wasn't a bad German after all, just an ordinary German, and he went to Bánovce nad Bebravou to look for Ladislav Hrobárik's wife Elena Hrobáriková. She was really surprised to hear the story regarding the digging but she agreed to do it.

But the thing is, Gusto Rúhe told the story the other way round and said that she was meant to keep everything they found there, and he was meant to keep just the stone that was yellow and transparent and was called Moonstone.

So they started digging exactly half way between the wall of the house and the well, and they found a tin box, like the one they used to have in grocery shops for keeping cloves. I don't mean cloves of garlic, but the kind of cloves that are used as spices. They are just both called cloves. But they're not cloves of garlic.

But what they found in the tin wasn't cloves that are used as spices but two small packages. In the first package they found a gun that had been taken apart and oiled, six gold rings, four gold watches and one case for glasses. Only instead of the glasses there were 4,500 dollars in the case. Except that the dollars were nine years out of date.

In the other package they didn't find anything except the Moonstone.

Elena Hrobáriková was very grateful but she decided to burn all the dollars just to be on the safe side, because in those days we still had the Communist Party and dollars were forbidden. And then she took the gun apart into even smaller pieces and buried it in the countryside because nobody ever went there.

So old Gusto Rúhe ended up with the Moonstone and he was really happy about that. But the thing was, the Moonstone didn't work and it never made any wishes come true and old Gusto Rúhe got very concerned. And to make things worse, someone later told old Gusto Rúhe that there was a bank in America where the money was valid for ten years after it stopped being valid.

So he got very upset about having been so stupid because he could have had 4,500 dollars and a gun and all those things made of gold but instead he ended up with a Moonstone. So he got even drunker than ever, and he kept drinking for three days in a row without getting sober and telling everyone in the Pub how he was supposed to get a thing that could make every wish come true and what an idiot he'd been regarding this.

People were surprised to hear this and wanted to have a look at the Moonstone. And as old Gusto Rúhe held it in his hands, he suddenly felt that due to the Moonstone he could tell the fortune regarding the person who had last held it in their hand before him.

The only problem was that he had to be drunk because he couldn't tell fortunes when he was sober.

So that's why he was drunk all the time and never got a job because of being drunk. And then he came to live in Komárno because his sister lived here and he moved in with her.

She was really unhappy about him not having a job and drinking alcoholic drinks all the time so she decided to go to the Communist Party to ask them to sort him out. So they sent this man whose name was Erik Rak to sort him out, because he was a policeman and was really good at sorting things out, but old Gusto Rúhe put such a bad spell on him that afterwards everyone was scared and nobody dared to sort Rúhe out.

Later on I will write about how old Gusto Rúhe put a spell on Erik Rak.

So Gusto Rúhe spent the rest of his life sitting outside the Pub by the Railway Station telling everyone that he got his just punishment regarding having lied to Elena Hrobáriková. And he kept asking people to buy him alcoholic drinks.

He kept saying that he hated the Moonstone and he kept urinating into the Floral Display and people were scared and disgusted, especially regarding his lower lip that was totally blue and hanging down to his chin.

Anyway.

Once I asked Alf Névéry if he wanted to have his fortune told, and he said that he didn't but he went to have a look at old Gusto Rúhe just the same. He did have a look but didn't want to have his fortune told and that's what I don't get, because what was the point of going to see old Gusto Rúhe and not getting his fortune told, right?

Right.

But Alf Névéry was really weird in all sorts of ways because he didn't have a job and never did anything, even though he didn't have a disability pension and he didn't even have a TV set.

When I found out about that, I got really scared because I'd never met anyone who didn't have a TV set in my whole life, or at any other time. And also because the reason he didn't have a TV set wasn't due to being poor, but because that's what he was like.

And the reason I know this is that when I found out about him not having a TV set, I told him that Szállási Jr was selling a TV set for just 500 Slovak crowns and I could deliver it on my handcart for free; that's when Alf Névéry told me that the reason why he didn't have a TV set was not because he couldn't afford one but because he didn't want one.

And that was really weird. Because everyone has a TV set, even Ivana who is a great artist in Bratislava has one, and Margita and her sons have one, and everyone in the world has one, only Alf Névéry didn't have one, and it wasn't because he couldn't afford it.

That was really weird but also really scary because you never know what's what and why and how and what might happen if you rent out to a person who has no TV set, because people might get all sorts of ideas about why he has no TV.

But the one thing I don't get is what he was up to all night long if he didn't watch TV. That was very weird and I told Ivana that I thought it was very weird that he didn't have a TV set because everyone has got one. But Ivana didn't care at all and every time she came they talked about foreign words and never about why he didn't have a TV set. Even though everybody has got one.

Even that rat-woman Angelika Édesová has got one, and she's a Gypsy. Even she's got a TV set. That's why it was very weird.

When he died I told Ivana it was no wonder that he died because maybe he wasn't right in the head, but he didn't know it because nobody had told him.

Because it's really very weird that he didn't have a TV set.

I never told anyone that we were renting to someone who didn't have a TV set, because people might have wondered why we were renting to someone like that. And I wouldn't have known what to say, because otherwise he was very tidy, except that he took too many showers and drank alcohol and kept his lights on all night.

Otherwise he had lots of good qualities.

Except that he didn't have a TV set.

Once there was this man in Komárno whose name was Ženge and he stole 22 TV sets in one go. Not because he needed 22 TV sets in one go, but because he made a plan. The plan Ženge made went like this:

He rang up the Communist Party High Ups in Komárno and said that it had been discovered that some TV sets made in the German Democratic Republic were faulty regarding people's health and that they would have to be taken away. But it had to be done in all secrecy, without alarming the Working Classes, and it was the law for the High Ups to get everything ready in complete secrecy. So they did as they were told and when Ženge came along with his driver and a lorry they had everything ready and packed and had even prepared refreshments, because they thought that Ženge was one of the High Ups, too.

After the refreshments Ženge made them all sign a piece of paper that said it was all a big Communist Party secret and they wouldn't tell anyone, otherwise they would all be in big trouble and they would end up in jail.

So they helped Ženge load the TV sets onto the lorry and he left all refreshed.

And after that Ženge had a good laugh because he thought it was very funny. But the thing was, his driver was that nasty raving queer Borka and he went around bragging about it so everyone knew all about it.

I knew all about it, too.

So I went to see Karol Gunár (PhD Social Sciences) and I told him everything because I always notice everything and that's why I knew about this, too Because if I hadn't told him it would have been a total disaster for the Communist Party, and then people would have made fun of them.

So they went and caught Ženge along with Borka and put them straight in jail and it serves them right. They got eight years each, even though they didn't manage to sell anything, because they stole the TV sets and made fun of the High Ups. And they gave German Democratic TV sets a bad name, too.

His name was Tihamér Ženge.

And after that Karol Gunár (PhD Social Sciences) praised me very much and he said that I was really clever because I always noticed everything and that I knew everything due to that. He told me to keep noticing things, but I don't need anyone to tell me that because I'm good at noticing things anyway because I've got I.Q.

Because I was the only one in the whole Market Place who noticed that something was wrong with Ján Boš-Mojš Jr when he fell down and his hand started shaking. But I noticed and I said straight away that something had to be done about it. I would have done something about it myself, but I'm not supposed to get worked up, because it's bad for me regarding my health.

And then this man came along who had two earrings in one ear and said he was a doctor and that it was an elyptical fit. Then he asked us for a stick or something hard but we couldn't find anything like that. So this man who said he was a doctor grabbed a carrot from a market stall and stuck it between Ján Boš-Mojš Jr's teeth.

It was very funny but nobody laughed because it was very serious, too.

That's why I didn't laugh either.

Then an ambulance came and took Ján Boš-Mojš Jr away along with the carrot and the man who said he was a doctor and had two earrings in one ear.

I don't know why he had to stick a carrot between his teeth but sometimes I think that maybe he did it regarding the elypsis because that's a serious illness.

And because carrots are very good for you.

Other vegetables are good for you too, but yoghurt is best of all. Yoghurt is the best thing for your health in the whole world. Every evening I always drink yoghurt and every morning I drink marsh-mallow herbal tea, because it's very good regarding clearing mucous obstruction from the system. But the thing is, you have to drink it very slowly so I drink it slowly because I've got plenty of time in the morning and otherwise the tea doesn't work.

I don't have to shave in the morning due to this illness that has a proper name and makes you stop growing and stops your beard growing and that's very handy, because it saves me time and I don't need to buy shaving things either.

That's why it's very handy.

And another thing that's handy is that shaving things make great presents for people who shave, like Valent Anka and his sons or Žebrák except that he doesn't have any sons, only daughters, so shaving things don't make good presents for them.

But shaving things are very handy.

Slippers make great presents for Ivana and Margita. Except that slippers are very expensive nowadays. When we still had the Communist Party, slippers were very cheap. But I don't blame them because I don't want them to think that I'm blaming them for being expensive. Even though it's true.

Slippers are very expensive.

Anyway.

At Christmas Ivana always gives me all sorts of silly clothes which I never ever wear but Margita gives me pyjamas and underwear which I wear. It was Margita who gave me the underpants called Panther that have a black animal embroidered on the leg.

In the old days we always used to get all together at Christmas, including Grandmummy and Grandaddy and Uncle Otto, and Mum and Dad, and Margita and Ivana.

I used to get all together at Christmas, too.

And we used to put the presents on the piano, because that's where the Christmas Tree used to be, and after dinner Ivana would play Christmas Carols and we would all sing along. I used to sing along too, although I don't really sing much because Christmas Carols are hard to remember because you only get to sing them at Christmas. And what's the point of singing Christmas Carols when it's not Christmas, right?

Right.

My favourite Christmas Carol used to be the one that goes like this:

'The holly bear's a berry
As red as blood.'

And then it goes like this:

'The holly bear's a bark
As bitter as gall.'

The only problem was that I had no idea what a holly bear was and why it was bitter or why it barked. Nobody told me what a holly bear was so I thought it was a normal bear, only it ate berries. And the berries were bitter and that made the holly bear bark.

Otherwise the holly bear was just like a normal bear. Except that it barked.

I already used to give people shaving things and slippers for Christmas in the old days because it was very handy and I was well-off regarding money already.

Because I've always been collecting lots of waste paper for Recycling even outside of paper collection time because it was really nice and it was interesting work. When I wasn't at school all I did was collect waste paper because it was really nice and interesting.

I finished all nine years of schooling and I never had to repeat a year because I've always been respected due to being so hard-working, and due to always coming top regarding waste paper.

Later on Karol Gunár (PhD Social Sciences) made sure that I kept going to school and never had to repeat a year so that I could stay in the same form as Darinka Gunárová and would always tell him everything that I noticed because I'm very good at noticing.

I've always been very good at noticing and every time I noticed something I would tell him because I have lots of good qualities and I've always got a lot of praise due to that.

I used to be friends with lots of people, too.

But I was mostly friends with Tonko Szedílek because he was my only friend.

Except that he had superstitious prejudices, meaning that he believed in religion and that wasn't allowed back then even though it's the law now. But back then, if you had a lot of superstitious prejudices, people would notice and so would the High Ups and it was a total disaster. That's why Grandaddy didn't me want me to play with Tonko, because he was worried that I would start believing in religion, too Because the games I used to play with Tonko were a bit weird, and he used to tell me all sorts of weird things regarding religion.

But what he mostly talked about was his Father and how he would come one day and then he would be on earth and everyone would be fine, especially Tonko because he was his son, but I would be fine too because I was his friend. I asked if Darinka Gunárová would be fine too, but Tonko said that he wasn't interested in Darinka Gunárová.

And then he told me that he talked to his Father every night about what it was like Up There but he didn't mean that his Father was High Up in the Communist Party, only that he was Up There. And every time he said Up There he turned up his head and pointed his chin upwards.

Sometimes I think that he was just making it up because he had superstitious prejudices. And besides, how could he talk to his Father who was Up There when Tonko was down here, right?

Right?

Later on Karol Gunár (PhD Social Sciences) also told me that Tonko had made it all up because he and Katuša Szedíleková had been born out of bedlock.

But then again, sometimes I still remember the weird smell that I could smell that night when I woke up. Only I had no idea where this smell came from because nobody explained to me what this smell was about and where it came from. And besides, Tonko had been born out of bedlock and due to that he wasn't right in the head and so it goes without saying that it was just his problem and that it isn't our problem, right?

Right.

Because it's true that Tonko had superstitious prejudices regarding religion.

Once there was this man in Komárno who also had superstitious prejudices regarding religion, and his name was Ľudovít Bucz. He was a driver regarding ambulances. And he had superstitious prejudices regarding the Protestant religion. But apart from the Protestant religion he was OK. He had religion on his mind all the time and he went to Church all the time but his wife was Catholic, not Protestant, and she never went to Church with him. Not because she was Catholic, but because she used to do sexual things with a man who was a Lieutenant Colonel in the Military while Ľudovít Bucz was at Church. Ľudovít Bucz didn't know about it, because he was more interested in Protestant things than sexual things, but once he came back from Church early because he had a cough and a temperature and wanted to go to bed. And that's where he found his wife with this man who was a Lieutenant Colonel in the Military.

But they didn't notice him because they were preoccupied.

So Ľudovít Bucz decided to do something about it. He went to Hospital, got one of the ambulances and crashed it into their house at full speed because their bedroom was on the street side. But they were fine because they were in the bathroom but Bucz wasn't fine because he died due to crashing the ambulance into his house. The ambulance got wrecked due to the crashing, too And then Mrs Buczová got into big trouble.

People said it served her right and they felt sorry for Ľudovít Bucz.

I felt sorry for him, too.

Then the man who was a Lieutenant Colonel in the Military also died due to suicide, but nobody felt sorry for him even though he shot himself in his own office with his own gun, because that's allowed in the Military.

His name was Lieutenant Colonel Peter Radosť (PhD Engineering).

I didn't do Military Service because I was excepted due to being disabled, but I wasn't happy about being excepted, not like some other people who were happy to be excepted because they didn't want to do Military Service. But the thing I don't get is why they were so happy to be excepted because it meant that they wouldn't have funny stories to tell about Military Service afterwards, because those who didn't get excepted always had lots of funny stories to tell about Military Service.

Žebrák was excepted from Military Service more than anyone else I've ever known because he's an artist and that's what they're all like. They all want to be excepted, but I don't get it, because if they didn't they could have all these funny stories to tell on TV and in newspapers and everyone would have a good laugh. Right?

Right.

Žebrák was excepted because he was very unhappy about doing Military Service. So he asked Uncle Otto if he knew a medicine against doing Military Service and Uncle Otto said he would think about it.

So he went and thought about it and the next time Žebrák came to Komárno Uncle Otto gave him some mushrooms that looked like bits of dirty glass, wrapped in a newspaper. Uncle Otto said that if he didn't want to do Military Service he would have to swallow as many of the mushrooms as he could fit into his mouth in one go, and he had to do that three times a day.

The name of the mushrooms that looked like bits of dirty glass was Blackshard Shapka. Uncle Otto told him that the Blackshard Shapka would make him look very ill regarding his urine but that it would be just black colour with a little bit of blood mixed in it. He said that his urine would turn black like the colour black.

So that's what Žebrák did and his urine did turn black like the colour black and the doctors were really astonished regarding his urine because they could only find a little bit of blood in it and every time they said he was OK, Žebrák would swallow as many Blackshard Shapkas as he could fit into his mouth and his urine would come out black as the colour black again.

In the end the doctors were so astonished that they said he didn't have to do Military Service.

Žebrák was very happy and so was Ivana, because they already had a baby, because Ivana kept having babies. And my Dad was happy too because they had pulled a trick on the army. But he didn't say it like that, he said it in very rude words.

I was happy too but I was also scared of getting into trouble, so I wasn't really happy.

After that Žebrák was very fond of Uncle Otto and after Uncle Otto went missing he even wrote a song about him because he's popular, not like Ivana.

And ever since Uncle Otto went missing, every time Žebrák comes to Komárno, he asks if there's any news of Uncle Otto.

And I always tell him there's no news. Because most people think we'll never hear from him because Uncle Otto is never going to come back. Margita says so too and she knows lots of people, so she should know.

After Žebrák ate the Blackshard Shapka mushrooms Ivana told me that if anyone found out what had happened regarding the Blackshard Shapkas, Žebrák would end up in jail, and so would Ivana, Uncle Otto, Dad, Mum as well as me, and that goes without saying.

So I got frightened that Karol Gunár (PhD Social Sciences) might find out about it, because the High Ups always used to find out about everything, and then I'd get into trouble regarding having known about it and not having reported it. That's why I went to see Karol Gunár (PhD Social Sciences) and I told him everything, because he was my friend.

Karol Gunár (PhD Social Sciences) was my friend and he was very nice and kind and he always listened to everything I had to say and he always gave me Karlsbad Wafers. He said that I was a good boy for coming to tell him and that I should always come and report everything regarding Žebrák, Uncle Otto and other people, too.

And that's why I've always told him everything.

And I've always got a lot of praise as well as Karlsbad Wafers and all sorts of badges and sometimes even sandwiches.

But the next time I went to see Karol Gunár (PhD Social Sciences) he said he had checked it all out and found out that Žebrák was really ill regarding coloured urine and not regarding Blackshard Shapkas, but that I should keep noticing things anyway and shouldn't tell anyone because it was our big secret. But he didn't have to tell me that, because I know how to keep a secret because I'm no retard. Right?

Right.

But the thing is, when Žebrák came to Komárno along with Ivana some time later, the police and the doctors came to ask him all sorts of questions including about Uncle Otto and his Mission and then everyone in my family got worked up and scared about what might happen and what was what and why and how, and Ivana shouted at me and said she would give me a right thrashing if it was me who told that stuck-up Gunár about it, but I didn't tell her anything about having reported it because I had promised Karol Gunár (PhD Social Sciences) that I wouldn't tell anyone.

Because a Young Pioneer knows how to keep a secret.

And another thing that Ivana told me was that if the High Ups ever found out, we would all end up in jail and that would include me because of aiding and abetting.

But I knew that I didn't do any aiding and abetting and if anyone ended up in jail it wouldn't be me, because I was friends with Karol Gunár (PhD Social Sciences). Anyway.

But the one thing I don't get is how come that back then it was such a big secret that the police had to come and ask Žebrák all those questions about avoiding, and how come that later, after the Communist Party was gone, Ivana once went on TV, except that she didn't play the piano but just sat there telling funny stories about her life? And she told the big secret about Žebrák and the Blackshard Shapkas on TV and it made everyone laugh because it was humorous. And I was the only one who didn't laugh, because I didn't think it was humorous at all.

Because the one thing I really hate is how everything can change just like that, and then from one day to the next everything can be different and nobody will tell you what's what and why and how, and you might think that everything is just like it used to be, but nothing is like it used to be and people can make fun of you because you don't know what's what and why and how.

Because that's what people are like.

And another thing I don't get is why Ivana has to be on TV all the time, and why she always has to push herself everywhere and say things on TV and in newspapers, as if she was something special.

I'm always scared of what Ivana might say next because she keeps saying things that you're not supposed to say.

Because that's what Ivana is like. Anyway.

But after the police came to ask Žebrák all these questions they sent him back to hospital for another test and after that Žebrák said that he would rather do Military Service than go for another test like that.

And when it was all over he told me to come to the kitchen and started telling me all about this test and how painful it was and when I heard it I nearly got sick, because I'm not supposed to get upset, so I told Žebrák to stop telling me about it but he wouldn't stop and he kept telling me all about it. How they tied him to a table and started sticking in a needle with a rubber tube attached. They were sticking it in there. You know where I mean. In his penis.

I don't know what the point was of Žebrák telling me all that. And I have no idea why he had to keep looking me in the eye as he was telling me how a doctor had held him down and another doctor stuck a needle with a tube attached in there. Sometimes I still have to think about Žebrák and how he sat in the kitchen looking me in the eye and telling me all about them sticking a needle with a tube you know where. In his penis.

I wanted to report him to Karol Gunár (PhD Social Sciences) and tell him how he had looked me in the eye, but I didn't know what to say because I didn't know how to tell him about the looking in the eye so I didn't say anything. Because if you can't say something what's the point of saying it, right?

Right.

But it's also possible that Žebrák just made it all up regarding the needle and the tube and the two doctors. Maybe they did no such thing to him because I'm also sick with my kidneys, in fact I'm much sicker than Žebrák and no such thing has ever happened to me. I just get my blood and urine samples taken all the time because everyone respects me, not just people, but doctors, too.

And the authorities respect me too because I got my disability pension straight away, without having to go to Hospital even though other people had to stay in Hospital before they got their disability pension.

And since then my pension has been raised many times over, because people respect me.

I don't really have to go to Hospital but I go anyway, partly regarding salt-free lunches and partly I go there on Tuesdays because I'm allowed to collect every Tuesday. But only cardboard, because you're not allowed to take anything else out of the Hospital. Because the only thing you're allowed to take out of the Hospital is cardboard, but only the kind of cardboard that's allowed. Nothing else is allowed because it's strictly forbidden.

Like for example the stuff in the blue sacks, that's not allowed because the blue sacks are full of all sorts of leftovers with germs in them and if they were taken out it would be a total disaster. Because the blue sacks would make everyone sick.

There's this security man at the Hospital whose name is Viliam Sásky and he always checks my handcart to make sure that I'm not taking out anything that's not allowed, because he's a very important person. But he is nice because he doesn't let other people take things out of the Hospital, he only allows me because he knows that I only take out things that are allowed. For example, Viliam Sásky won't let that rat-woman Angelika Édesová, the nasty Gypsy, to take things out because he knows that she would take out the sacks with the leftovers, because people like her don't care if it's allowed or not.

When I go home from hospital sometimes I stop and sit in the little park by the Water Tower. The one that Tonko Szedílek fell from. But I don't like to sit there very much, because I don't like to think about it.

Because I got a lot of praise afterwards and people said that I was a clever boy. Especially Karol Gunár (PhD Social Sciences), he gave me a lot of praise and said that I was a clever boy, only Darinka Gunárová didn't want to be my friend any more, and she became very weird.

Yesterday I saw Darinka Gunárová outside the Cultural Centre. When we met she shook hands with me just like I was a real person.

People don't usually shake hands with me very much, even though they respect me for being hard-working and whatever, but that's because I am usually out and about with my handcart and I have to hold the handle so that's why I don't usually shake hands with people.

I put some rubber foam around the handle in the winter to keep my hands warm because this is serious work and I can't always wear gloves because I wouldn't be able to tie knots on the ropes to stop the cardboard from falling off. Sometimes when my skin gets chapped, I treat it with Indulóna Lotion with Healing Power.

Indulóna Lotion with Healing Power is very good.

Anyway.

So Darinka Gunárová shook hands with me, but I didn't know what I was supposed to say so I just laughed and Darinka Gunárová laughed, too.

But her name isn't Darinka Gunárová any more because she's married to a black man now. Her black husband's name is Samuel Quentin, like mine. I don't mean that my name is Samuel Quentin like his because my name is Samuel Tále. Because I'm not black, I'm Slovak.

A long time ago I heard people say that Darinka Gunárová had married a black man in America but I didn't believe them, because people often make up things like that, and they used to gossip about Darinka when she was still married to that fat slob Manica. They already gossiped about her then. I never gossiped about Darinka Gunárová, either when she was married to that fat slob Manica or at any other time.

I hated that fat slob Manica because he was the first one in Komárno to shout at me like this:

'Everybody thinks
Samko Tále stinks.'

He shouted like that even before he married Darinka, just because he felt like it.

So that's why I didn't believe it when I heard that she had married a black man, because even that fat slob Manica was white, not black.

And besides, nobody in Komárno had ever married a black person before. Because there are enough Slovaks around, right?

Right.

But then I saw him with my own eyes. It was when Darinka Gunárová's Mum died and I went to her funeral. Of course it goes without saying that I didn't go there because I wanted to see Darinka Gunárová and her husband the black man. That's out of the question. I went there out of respect because Karol Gunár (PhD Social Sciences) was my friend. And that's when I saw that he was a real black man.

Just like on TV.

Because I've seen lots of black men on TV before but this one was really real, not like on TV. He was really black. And he was almost as tall as my Grandfather from Detva even though he was black.

But the thing is, my Grandfather from Detva was white and all the real people who are for real and not on TV are white. Except for Gypsies, but they don't count because they are Gypsies.

Once there was this man in Komárno whose name was Harry H. Torry, but he wasn't from Komárno, he was from America. And he wasn't black, he was white, just as if he was from Komárno. That's how white he was. Just like people from Komárno. He was a teacher regarding English lessons because that's the law now.

Harry H. Torry was a teacher in a school for normal children but that wasn't enough for him, so he went to Gypsy schools and gave Gypsy children English lessons for free.

There's just one thing I don't get: what was the point of giving them English lessons, surely it's enough for them to speak Gypsy to steal my cardboard from the Market Place, right?

Right.

But this Harry H. Torry kept saying that Gypsies were suppressed in Komárno regarding being Gypsies, and he kept saying that all people were equal and that Slovaks were just like Gypsies. But it wasn't a good idea to say things like that, even though he came from America and people respected him due to that, because when he said that Slovaks were just like Gypsies people got offended and didn't want him to teach their children any more.

I got offended, too.

Because nobody wants to be all equal with Gypsies, and that's why he had to go back to America earlier than he planned. As he was leaving, he packed all his bags and suitcases and his tennis racket and went to say goodbye to his Gypsies and while he was saying goodbye, the Gypsies stole all his bags and suitcases as well as his tennis racket.

So Harry H. Torry went to the police and told them what had happened and the police had a good laugh and said that now he could see what the difference was between a Gypsy and a Slovak. Then they got in a police car and took him around the Gypsy houses and in one hour they got all his things back, except for his tennis racket because the Gypsies had already burned it because they had a fire.

And then the people were happy and thought that Harry H. Torry now understood the difference between Gypsies and Slovaks, but I don't think he understood anything because he kept saying that there was no difference. And after that people weren't happy any more and Harry H. Torry had to leave again. And when he got back to America he wrote to all the newspapers about people in Slovakia being racial.

But the one thing I don't get is why he wrote that people in Slovakia were racial because it wasn't the people who stole his bags and his suitcases as well as his tennis racket, it was the Gypsies, right?

Right.

I'm not racial at all because I'm very nice.

And the way you can tell is because whenever I watch a film on TV and someone in the film is racial towards Red Indians or slaves, I get very angry about them being racial, and if they get punished it makes me very happy.

I don't know if Alf Névéry was racial or not because he didn't have a TV set so we couldn't talk about it. If he'd had a TV set I would have known.

Margita and Valent Anka aren't racial either, because we don't have any Red Indians or slaves in Komárno. Maybe they have some in Bratislava, so maybe Ivana is racial but I don't know about that.

Because she's very weird and she and Žebrák never complain about Hungarians or Czechs, but it goes without saying that the reason why they don't complain is because Žebrák's father was a Czech. Otherwise I'm sure they would complain, because if you don't complain people might notice and they wouldn't trust you any more because you would be suspicious.

I'm not suspicious because I complain.

But I never complain about Red Indians or slaves because I'm not racial.

Once there was this man in Komárno whose name was Otrok which means slave in Slovak, but it was just his name, not his job. He was a slave by name, not by profession. His name was Štefan Otrok but people called him Pišta Otrok because that's what you say in Hungarian if somebody's name is Štefan. And he used to buy and sell feathers and his wife used to make duvets out of them. He had a car with a loudspeaker and he used to drive around town shouting through the loudspeaker about buying feathers and making duvets and that made him very popular. He was especially popular due to the humorous things regarding feathers and duvets that he used to say.

Some people used to follow his car just to hear what humorous things he was going to say regarding feathers and duvets. And sometimes, when he passed me in his car, he would say humorous things regarding me too through the loudspeaker and then I would also follow his car and shout at him like this:

'Otrok Pišta,
Shitty mister'

And everybody laughed because it was humorous.

Štefan Otrok laughed too and this is what he shouted into his loud-speaker:

'Everybody thinks
Samko Tále stinks.

And I laughed too, even though I don't like it but the loudspeaker made it sound humorous.

Then Štefan Otrok's wife ran off to Poland with a Polish man and left him here with all the feathers and duvets but Štefan Otrok gave it all up and stopped buying and making and saying humorous things.

His wife was 58 years old when she ran off. The Polish man was 38 years old. Štefan Otrok was 68 years old.

Everyone was disgusted at that.

I was disgusted at it,, too.

And after that Štefan Otrok went to an old people's home in Hurba-novo and I've never seen him since, because Hurbanovo is very far away.

Anyway.

I've never met any Polish men, but once I met a Polish woman whose name was Daryna Kamyk, because she once came up to me at the big crossroads outside the Hospital and asked if she could take my picture regarding being a journalist. Because she was very impressed to see me being so hard-working with my full handcart at the big crossroads outside the Hospital.

But I said I didn't want my picture taken because you never know what might happen and what's what and why and how, because people might say one thing and then they might do something quite different and you never know what might happen then. But everyone respects me so Daryna Kamyk can go and find somebody else to take a picture of at the big crossroads outside the Hospital.

Because you can't be too careful.

I am always very careful.

For example, I always double-check many times that the doors are locked to make sure they are locked. The same with my handcart. Because you can't be too careful, right? Right.

And then Daryna Kamyk gave me her business card which said:

Daryna Kamyk
Editor

Meaning that her name was Daryna Kamyk and that she was an editor.

Sometimes I wonder what might have happened if I had let Daryna Kamyk take my picture for her newspaper, and if I had gone to Poland. People there might have recognized me and said, hey, that's the man from Komárno who was so impressive at the big crossroads outside the Hospital, and all sorts of other things might have happened then.

But I don't have time for silly things like that and besides, Poland is a long way away.

I have kept her business card because not many people give me their business cards very often because people know me, and if somebody doesn't know me then what would be the point of giving me their business cards anyway, right?

Right.

But I've got Daryna Kamyk down in my Christian Names Notebook as well as in my Surnames Notebook because you never know. I haven't got anyone else called Kamyk in there, just her, and I've got only one Daryna. Because she's Daryna spelt with *Y*. I have two other Darinas whose names are spelt with *I* in my Christian Names Notebook. One is

Darina Ukrajčoková and she's a cleaner at the Market Place, and the other one is Darinka Gunárová.

Yesterday I saw Darinka Gunárová outside the Cultural Centre. And this is what she said:

'Samko, it's been fifteen years since I last saw you.'

Meaning it had been fifteen years since she last saw me.

But I didn't know what to say because it hadn't been fifteen years, it was only nine years since I saw her at her Mum's funeral where I also saw her husband, the black man.

But I didn't want to say that.

She was wearing a golden belt on top of her short skirt, and the belt was so wide that you could have made two belts out of it, and it was tightened really tight even though it's very bad for you. I know that because whenever Grandaddy wasn't feeling well, he would loosen his trousers and his shirt straight away and we had to keep very quiet because Grandaddy wasn't feeling well. And then Grandaddy would take these pills that you weren't supposed to swallow, you were just supposed to leave them under your tongue.

Honestly, you were supposed to leave those pills under your tongue and not swallow them. Because that's what you were supposed to do with those pills. I have no idea why under your tongue, because nobody ever explained to me how it worked under the tongue. But these pills were very important, because Grandaddy never went anywhere without them. He wouldn't even go to the Local Party Cell meeting without these pills.

After it all happened with Tonko regarding the Water Tower, Gran–daddy got really unwell and he had to lie down in the bedroom propped up on four pillows and he was so worked up that his fingers went all white and his nails went all blue as though he had dipped them in ink. But it goes without saying that he hadn't dipped them in ink and that he was just ill regarding his fingers.

And then he pointed one of his fingers at the lamp and said that if the High Ups got to know about it, they would do something about it and it would be a total disaster.

But what he meant was not the lamp, he meant the High Ups, because I'm no retard so I know that he didn't mean the lamp. Because a lamp is a lamp and it's not the High Ups even though it is high up, and nobody ever means a lamp when they mean the High Ups, so there.

Because that's out of the question.

Also later, when Grandaddy was in Hospital because he got cancer in there, you know where I mean, in his penis, he kept pointing upwards and saying that the High Ups would come back and that would be a total disaster. This was after the Communist Party had to leave and the Others came instead, and when Ivana and I went to see him in hospital Grandaddy got terribly worked up because Ivana had a flag in her buttonhole and what it meant in those days was that she didn't want the Communist Party and that she wanted the Others instead. And he whispered to her in a very worked up voice that she should take it off immediately. Because he couldn't shout any more due to the cancer.

And then he pointed his finger upwards again and said that we didn't know what they were like, but he knew exactly what they were like and that's why he knew that they were just testing us, and that they were going to come back and that would be a total disaster.

After that Ivana took the flag off to stop him getting worked up because he was already 89 years old and he was very ill anyway.

When we were out of the Hospital she pinned it back on, and after that Grandaddy died.

And we went to his funeral.

Everyone was very sad and everyone cried at his funeral, except Ivana didn't cry because I've never ever seen her cry, except that one time when she sat on the floor in the toilet regarding Alf Névéry and had tears and snot and saliva running down her face.

Anyway.

Margita cried more than anyone else in my family because she is very kind-hearted, and I cried a lot too but Ivana cried least of all because she is a great artist from Bratislava and she always wears dark glasses to funerals so that people couldn't tell if she cried or not and they were disappointed due to that.

I wasn't disappointed because I knew that Ivana didn't cry. Anyway.

When Grandmummy died it was Grandaddy who cried more than anyone else and people felt sorry for him and said, oh the poor man, look how sad he is. But the weirdest thing was that the louder Grandaddy cried the less my Mum and Uncle Otto cried. And later on, when it looked as if Grandaddy was about to jump into Grandmummy's grave, my Mum suddenly turned round and left. That was really weird and people wondered why she left the funeral before it was over, but my Mum said that she had to leave because she felt ill.

But sometimes I think that she didn't really feel ill and that she left due to something else because people kept giving her weird looks due to leaving before it was over. Because it's never happened in Komárno before that anyone left their own mother's funeral before it was over.

I didn't leave because I stayed till the end.

I've always stayed until the end of every funeral I've been to because I don't want to offend a dead person because I'm no retard and I know how to behave.

Because I'm no retard.

Because I'm just like everyone else and people respect me because I'm just like everyone else. Only Grandaddy used to say that there was some of Grandmummy's blood in the Boy and once when he got worked up regarding Grandmummy he said that Grandmummy's Grandmother wasn't just half Hungarian but that she was half Gypsy too, and that's why her name was Eszter Csonka.

But that can't be true at all and I hate it when people say things like that about Eszter Csonka being not just half Hungarian but half Gypsy on top of that, because that's not true and nobody in the whole world or in Slovakia can say things like that about Eszter Csonka being not just half Hungarian but half Gypsy, too.

That sort of thing ought to be forbidden.

And it ought to be possible to get a Certificate which I could have in the Documents so I could show to people to prove that I'm a proper Slovak just like every other Slovak, and also to stop people saying things like that about Eszter Csonka. And if they kept on saying things like that they would get reported and be in big trouble regarding a fine.

But one thing I don't get is why Grandaddy never said things like that about Ivana or Margita and about their blood even though Ivana has always been artistic regarding the piano and it goes without saying that many Gypsies are artistic regarding musical instruments. I've never been artistic regarding any musical instruments, and yet Grandaddy used to say things like that about me.

That's why I went to see Karol Gunár (PhD Social Sciences) and I told him what Grandaddy had said and Karol Gunár (PhD Social Sciences) was very nice and he said I was a good boy and Grandaddy must have been joking.

And that relieved me, because the Communist Party knows everything and if those things about Eszter Csonka had been true Karol Gunár (PhD Social Sciences) would have known about it. But he didn't know about it so it can't have been true.

And that relieved me.

Because if it had been true and there was some of that blood in me then Karol Gunár (PhD Social Sciences) wouldn't have respected me so much for being hard-working, right?

Right.

But there isn't any of that blood in me, so there.

Because I'm just like anyone else, because if I wasn't just like anyone else I would be totally different, but I'm not and I have my own one-bedroom flat and I look after it and I pay all my bills on time and can sort out everything by myself, even though I never sort out anything because Margita always sorts out everything for me. Because she knows lots of people regarding sending children to children's homes.

Plus I'm well-off regarding money too, because I'm very economical and I don't waste money on silly things such as alcohol and cigarettes and other stuff that's bad for you, because I only drink yoghurt and marsh-mallow herbal tea.

But yoghurt is the best.

Because yoghurt is very good for you. Anyway.

And that's why I only drink yoghurt and I never waste money on silly things, and due to that I'm well-off regarding money, too I keep my money in a Savings Account because you can't be too careful. I have a password, too I made up the password myself. But I won't write it down here because I can't be too careful, even though I'm a writer now. Because if I wrote it down here something might happen and even though I don't want to say anything bad about this man called Koloman Kertész Bagala because I don't even know him, I can't be too careful because you never know what might happen and what's what and why and how.

I was going to ask Ivana about him because she knows everyone but I didn't because she would have asked why I was asking because that's what she's like so I won't tell her.

She doesn't have any good qualities at all.

I have lots of good qualities and I'm very careful as well. That's why I'm not going to write down how well-off I am regarding money. When Margita's son Patrik was going to America, Margita wanted to borrow some money from Ivana but they had an argument regarding politics and afterwards she didn't want to ask her so she asked me instead to lend her 50,000 Slovak crowns in money so I gave her the money because I always eat lunch at their house on Sundays, and besides I didn't know how to tell her that I couldn't lend her the money and why. So I did. And after that her husband Valent Anka said that he was going to be fifty years old this year and he would throw a big party, like the Hungarians have never seen in Komárno, and that he would invite me, too.

But he needn't tell me things like that about inviting me to his party and whatever. I don't care about being invited because I don't have time for silly things like that and besides, he said that he was going to make hunter's goulash with spices and barrels of beer, but I'm not allowed hunter's goulash because it's very spicy and I'm not allowed beer either because it's very alcoholic.

And people would just stare at me anyway because all sorts of engineers from the Docks would be there but I'm very hard-working and I'm not allowed hunter's goulash because it's very spicy and because I have to take good care of myself.

And that's why it's totally out of the question.

What I would also like to know is if he's going to invite Ivana and Žebrák as well, because they always argue regarding politics. Last time they had an argument it was in my room for living, and they all stood round the table arguing with very long words. First Valent Anka said that he was an engineer in the Docks so he knew what life was about, but Ivana had no idea what life was about because all she did was jet-setting all round the world. Then Ivana said that she was jet-setting all round the world so she knew what life was about, but Valent Anka was just an engineer in the Docks and had no idea what life was about.

Then they said all sorts of long words to each other and after that Ivana left for Bratislava along with Žebrák and they have only met at funerals since then. And that's why I wonder if he's going to invite them to his party because Valent Anka's party will be a party, not a funeral.

But if Ivana keeps on being like that and if she keeps telling me off for being unhygienic, I will report her to Žebrák and he'll show her what's what.

Because I did report her to Karol Gunár (PhD Social Sciences) too and I reported to him how Ivana cried in the toilet, because in the old days Karol Gunár (PhD Social Sciences) told me that I should always report everything about Žebrák's military service and the Blackshard Shapka mushroom, so that's what I've always done. Because they've got to know everything, because if there was something they didn't know and the Communist Party came back and asked them how come they didn't know something, even though other people knew, it would be a total disaster.

That's why I reported everything about Ivana but all that Karol Gunár (PhD Social Sciences) said was that it was to be expected, that she had always been the first one to judge others and now she behaved like this.

Then he gave me some Poprad Wafers because he said that he wasn't buying Karlsbad Wafers any more, because we had to support our own wafers instead of Czech wafers.

I support our wafers instead of Czech wafers, too.

Because they are very tasty and they are very good for you.

Karol Gunár (PhD Social Sciences) also likes them because they are tasty and very good for you, plus they are Slovak and not Czech.

Anyway.

Yesterday I saw Darinka Gunárová outside the Cultural Centre. We shook hands and I laughed because I didn't know what's what and why and how, and Darinka Gunárová laughed too and then I didn't mind laughing either.

Darinka Gunárová was on her own and I was on my own too because people don't often walk with me in the street, because when I'm out and about with my handcart it's always loaded full of cardboard and I can't see what's ahead of me, so I need to make sure that I can see at least what's behind me, and that's why I had a rear-view mirror fitted on my handcart, only it's broken off now and I've become a writer due to that.

And what's also very important is that I'm a proper road user which means that I can't go round walking with people just like that because I'm a proper road user and I have to watch my step very carefully and due to that I had a rear-view mirror fitted on my handcart.

Once there was this man in Komárno whose name was Marián Merďoch and he was a policeman and he said that I had to have a hooter on my handcart, too Like the one people have in their cars for hooting. A hooter. So I asked Szálássi Jr to fit a hooter on my handcart but he just laughed and didn't want to do it, but I told him to, so he did. So now when I'm out and about with my handcart, I can go around hooting because I'm a road user and it's the law to hoot regarding being careful. I have to press a button on the handle but it's not the button that's broken now, so my hooter isn't broken. It runs on batteries and they need to be changed because they run out. They run out due to hooting regarding being careful.

Szállási Jr said that he could fit my handcart with a hooter that hooted a tune just like the one Ján Boš-Mojš sings when he says his name. But I didn't want that because I have nothing to do with Ján Boš-Mojš except that my handcart is in his workshop now and if I started hooting the same tune people might wonder why.

I might wonder why, too.

And this man Marián Merďoch, the one who was a policeman and told me to get a hooter regarding being careful, he had a sister whose name was Lívia and she was a teacher regarding school children at school, and once on May Day she got so drunk outside the House of Czechoslovak-Soviet Friendship that she went off and did it with two men at the same time. You know what I mean. Sexual things. And she did it right by the Funfair, so the schoolchildren saw her and this is what they shouted at her:

'Proletarian greetings, Comrade Teacher!'

But she didn't notice due to being drunk. Then one of the men who worked at the Funfair and had done time in jail telephoned Marián Merďoch the policeman, and told him what his sister was doing with two men at the same time, and Marián Merďoch came in his police car and put Lívia in the police car and drove her home. And then he put her on the ground in their front garden next to the well and threw some water on her and then he took off his belts and beat her until she woke up. He beat her with two belts at the same time.

When she woke up, she tried to crawl back into the house because people were looking over the fence but Merďoch didn't care because he was a policeman. And every time she fainted he pumped some more water on her and kept on beating her with the two belts.

Lívia Merďochová was wearing a Young Pioneer's outfit with a Young Pioneer's Scarf and when it got soaked with water the colour started running and her white Young Pioneer's shirt turned all red from the colour that ran off her red Young Pioneer's Scarf.

When he was done, Marián Merďoch left her in the front garden and went back on duty.

And the other people went home saying that this was something Lívia Merďochová would never forget.

I said so, too.

Maybe this really was something Lívia Merďochová never forgot but nobody could tell because after she recovered from all her fainting she stuttered so badly that she never managed to say a whole word for the rest of her life because all she could say was the beginning of a word.

And after that she never married, so she lived with her brother and she couldn't be a teacher regarding children either, due to the stutter. She was very modest and very hard-working and she never went out except to exhibitions sometimes because after all this happened to her she took up embroidery and her embroideries were so beautiful they were shown at embroidery exhibitions.

And people said that nobody in Komárno made embroideries as beautiful as Lívia Merďochová.

I said so, too.

One of her embroideries was shown as far as Canada and also on TV.

Lívia Merďochová's eyes were purple like nobody else's in the world. They were totally purple. Like the colour purple.

Every evening she used to go for a walk with her brother. When he was on duty she didn't go for a walk.

Anyway.

The only thing I don't get is why the colour of her Young Pioneer's Scarf ran so much because the colour of my Young Pioneer's Scarf never ran. But then again, mine wasn't properly red, it was sort of orange. But even if I left it to soak for two hours the colour never ran, not a bit.

My Young Pioneer's Scarf was very beautiful and very good.

Anyway.

Once I saw a film from America on TV and in this film there were all sorts of American soldiers and even gangsters wearing Young Pioneers' Scarves and I got very outraged when I saw that Americans were allowed to wear Young Pioneers' Scarves, too There was even a black man wearing a Young Pioneer's Scarf and that made me really very outraged.

Black people shouldn't be allowed to wear Young Pioneers' Scarves. That sort of thing is out of the question.

When I saw Darinka Gunárová's husband, the black man, he wasn't wearing a Young Pioneer's Scarf and that relieved me very much, but then again it was at a funeral and people wouldn't normally wear Young Pioneers' Scarves at funerals, so it goes without saying that he wasn't wearing one either.

Darinka Gunárová got out of the car wearing a dress that was all black and on her head she wore a hat with a black curtain. Her husband the black man was wearing a black suit. Darinka went with him arm-in-arm which means they were walking arm-in-arm. That's what Grandmummy used to say, arm-in-arm. Darinka went into the mortuary arm-in-arm. I stayed outside because I was just a bystander and not a mourner.

When Alf Névéry died I was meant to be only a bystander, too but Alf Névéry was all alone regarding his divorce and nobody would have been a mourner, so Ivana went and stood in front and she dragged me along and made me stand in front too as if I was a mourner.

I hate it when Ivana drags me. I want her to stop dragging me.

But that time I didn't know what to do so I went and stood behind the coffin even though I wasn't a mourner at all. Neither was Ivana but that's what she's like, always pushing herself everywhere.

Otherwise there were all sorts of people from Bratislava at Alf Névéry's funeral because he was very well-known, even though I don't really know people from Bratislava because I only know people from Komárno.

Because Bratislava is a long way away.

Actually, it was quite handy to be standing behind the coffin because that way I could have a good look at all these people because they were standing on the other side facing us.

Ivana wore dark glasses, because that's what she's like.

Another person I saw at the funeral was the fat slob Manica. I hate him because he was the first person to shout at me like this:

'Everybody thinks
Samko Tále stinks.'

And then I started shouting at him like this:

'Manica the slob
Couldn't find his knob.'

That made everyone laugh and Manica was embarrassed. Serves him right, that fat slob Manica.

I don't know what he was doing at Alf Névéry's funeral and I'll never know because I won't ever ask him. I'm not asking that fat slob Manica anything and he can go to Alf Névéry's funeral every day for all I care, that fat slob Manica.

He was Darinka Gunárová's first husband and they got married when they were sixteen years old, because Manica was our classmate too, but that was before he became a fat slob. Now he's very fat. He's so fat that the lowest of his chins rests on his tie.

I haven't got fat at all because I have a very healthy life of style.

After he and Darinka Gunárová got divorced, he married Valent Anka's sister whose name was Anka Anková. So now the fat slob Manica is my relative, because we're related now. But I never say hello to him and he doesn't say hello to me either, so why should I say hello to him? After all, he was the first to start shouting at me like this:

'Everybody thinks
Samko Tále stinks.'

But I don't stink at all and it's out of the question that I should stink because I'm very hygienic and whatever. I hate Manica because afterwards other people also started shouting at me like that so then I started shouting at Manica like this:

'Manica the slob
Couldn't find his knob.'

Actually, I have no idea if he could find it or not because I'm not a queer, but it was very funny and Manica was embarrassed about not finding his knob. Meaning you know what. His penis.

And it serves him right.

Now he works in this office regarding people who are unemployed and get paid for not working.

I work every day even though I have a disability pension, but some people don't work at all even though they attended all sorts of schools and they get paid for not working.

The only thing I don't get is why they get paid when they're not working. When we still had the Communist Party nobody got paid for not working and everybody went to work. And nobody was paid due to unemployment back then.

I was never paid due to unemployment either.

Not everyone in my family has worked but that wasn't due to unemployment, that was due to disability. My Mum was disabled due to her bad back, Uncle Otto was disabled due to the lightning, and I was disabled due to kidneys, but all of us have always worked because we're very hard-working. Except for Uncle Otto who didn't work, but that was because he had a Mission, but at least he went gathering mushrooms. My Mum used to work regarding giving lessons to children and the children used to pay her twenty Czechoslovak crowns per lesson because that was when we still had Czechoslovakia so the money was called Czechoslovak crowns. But then Grandaddy said that it wasn't allowed and that we could get into big trouble because my Mum had a disability pension and she got paid twenty Czechoslovak crowns per lesson, so he told my Mum to ask the children to bring eggs, vegetables or fruit and whatever per lesson. So my Mum asked them to.

But then this girl who used to come to my Mum for piano lessons and whose name was Eva-Mária Kisstóthová came to her lesson with a handcart and she brought an old chair that had only three legs and she said that's what her parents had sent. My Mum got really worked up and she started to cry and sent Eva-Mária Kisstóthová home with the chair.

And after that she told the children to bring twenty Czechoslovak crowns per lesson.

But the one thing I don't get is why she got so worked up, because my Dad was really clever regarding woodworking and he could easily have fixed that chair and then we would have had another chair and that would have been very handy. Because we only had five chairs, because there were five of us, and when Margita got married to Valent Anka it wasn't handy any more, because we were always having to bring another chair from another room.

And that wasn't handy at all.

I have three chairs in my kitchen because there isn't room for more and that's very handy, too.

I don't often have many visitors because I don't have time for silly things like that, and that's why three chairs are just right for my kitchen.

Alf Névéry never came to visit me very often because it was always me who used to go and visit him when I felt like visiting him. And he used to give me Karlsbad Wafers because he didn't support Slovak wafers. But he never ate them himself because he never ate, he just drank alcoholic drinks.

Once I found him writing something so I asked if he was going to become a writer again and he said that he would never be a writer again because he had figured it all out.

But he never told me what it was that he had figured out, so I don't have any idea what it was he had figured out, but I still think that it's very weird because it should go without saying that if he'd figured it all out, that's exactly why he should have become a writer, right?

Right.

For example, I became a writer because I figured out that I had to take my handcart to Ján Boš-Mojš's workshop. But I still have no idea what it was that he had figured out, because he never told me. Sometimes I keep wondering all the time what he meant. Because it's very weird and I don't know why he never wanted to become a writer after he'd figured it all out.

It's very weird.

Once Ivana came to see me, except that she didn't come to see me, she came to see Alf Névéry, but I was there as well because you never know what might happen and what's what and why and how, so you have to be very careful, and that's why I am always very careful, and then he said that if he ever wrote anything it would have a title that would go like this:

The Mortuary
A Life of Vain Glory

I had a good laugh because it was humorous when he said: 'The Mortuary, A Life of Vain Glory' but Ivana didn't laugh and Alf Névéry didn't laugh either. But I don't get it because what is the point of making up humorous sentences if you're not going to laugh at them?

So then I didn't laugh either.

Because if nobody is laughing it can't really be humorous, right?

Right.

Because the way I can always tell that something is humorous is because it makes people laugh. Ivana can never tell and she doesn't care if other people are laughing or not even though she attended all sorts of schools and keeps pushing herself onto TV.

At least Margita doesn't push herself onto TV because her job is just regarding sending children to children's homes. I don't know if Valent Anka is pushing himself or not, because he was on TV only once and he talked about how suppressed we are by the Hungarians because we live in the South of Slovakia.

But the most important thing was that when they showed the names of all the people that had been on TV that night they put Valent Anča instead of Valent Anka and then all the people in the Docks started calling him Anča and he has been insulted and injured ever since because Anka sounds like you're being nice to a girl called Anka, but Anča sounds like you're being nasty to her. Later he said that the people on TV did it on purpose because he dared to criticize Hungarians and there are Hungarians everywhere, even on TV and in Bratislava.

Because Hungarians are everywhere. Especially in Komárno, even though I have no idea why they are here, nobody told me anything about it so how should I know? There are also lots of Hungarians in Hungary and nobody minds that. But what people really mind is that they are in Komárno too and that we are all very suppressed due to them.

I am very suppressed due to them, too.

And another person who is very suppressed due to them is Valent Anka because they insulted and injured him regarding making fun of his name and calling him Anča on TV.

Once there was this man in Komárno but he wasn't from Komárno, he was from Marhaň which is a village, except I don't know where it is. His name was Daniel Gaby and he did his Military Service in Komárno because we have Military Service, too And all the other soldiers made fun of him because his name Gaby sounded like he was a woman called Gaby. Except that he wasn't a woman, he just had a surname that was like a woman's first name.

At first he thought it was funny too and he didn't let on that it bothered him that people spoke to him as if he was a woman. Because what they kept saying to him were things like this:

'How many men have you screwed today, Gaby?'

Everything would have worked out all right except that one night he put on his full uniform on top of his pyjamas, then he put on his shoes and everything else and started hitting the door with his fist and shouting:

'Give it to him, knock him out, finish him off!'

All the other people woke up and started laughing because they thought it was funny but then they stopped because they realized that it wasn't funny and they had to call all sorts of people including a doctor and he said that Daniel Gaby had gone mad. He got really, really mad and they had to put him in the madhouse.

And after that Daniel Gaby was in the madhouse and nobody has heard of him since, because he was in the madhouse.

I've never heard of him either.

Once I asked old Gusto Rúhe if Daniel Gaby was still in the madhouse and he asked me for an alcoholic drink and this is what he chalked on the tarmac after that:

'Big bullshit.'

I have no idea what Gusto Rúhe meant by big bullshit so I asked him what he meant by big bullshit but he never tells anyone's fortune twice even if you buy him two shots of alcohol because that's what he's like, so I have no idea what he meant by big bullshit regarding Daniel Gaby.

Old Gusto Rúhe has never written anything that made any sense, except once, when I asked him if Uncle Otto would ever come back. He asked me to get him an alcoholic drink and this is what he chalked on the tarmac:

'Never.'

After that I thought that maybe I shouldn't have asked him because there was really no need for old Gusto Rúhe to put it like this: 'Never'. He could just as easily have just written: 'Don't know', right?

Right.

I don't believe anything that old Gusto Rúhe writes on the tarmac in front of the Pub anyway, because he's an alcoholic and his lower lip hangs all the way down to his chin. But there was no need to write: 'Never', right?

Right.

Once Ivana went to see him too but she wouldn't tell me why she wanted her fortune told, but I told her that she shouldn't go to see him because he never tells women's fortunes unless they let him grope them but that's what Ivana is like, she thinks she's a great artist from Bratislava and that he will tell her fortune without groping. But everything happened exactly like I said, because I always know everything because I know.

But Ivana didn't let him grope her so he didn't grope her and due to that she didn't have her fortune told, but she gave him 50 Slovak crowns anyway and ever since then old Gusto Rúhe always asks me when my sister will be in town again because he spent all that money on an alcoholic drink straight away. And I always tell him to mind his own business. But I don't say it in nice words, I say it in rude words.

But the thing is, that's what Ivana is like and I bet that the next time she comes to town she will go and see old Gusto Rúhe again and then she will talk about him everywhere because she keeps pushing herself in everywhere.

Margita would never go to see him because she finds him disgusting because he stinks and she always says that he just sits there and nobody does anything about it and he's an embarrassment to the whole town due to his stinking, but one thing that makes Margita happy regarding old Gusto Rúhe is that he's not Slovak even though he comes from Banská Štiavnica, because he is German and so nobody can say that he is Slovak which means that he isn't an embarrassment to Slovaks, only to Germans regarding wetting himself.

Otherwise there aren't many Germans in Komárno, just lots of Hungarians and Gypsies and also some Vietnamese, especially in the Market Place but the Vietnamese are nice because they don't push other people around and they don't speak Vietnamese. I mean they do speak Vietnamese but only among themselves. But Hungarians speak Hungarian even when they are not among themselves.

But people forgive the Vietnamese for speaking Vietnamese because we have never been suppressed by them. And that's why they are allowed in Slovakia. We have always been suppressed by the Hungarians and that's why we will never forgive them. That goes without saying, right?

Right.

Except that Ivana doesn't care and she even defends them and that's really embarrassing. I don't see what the point was of her having attended all sorts of schools and going to all sorts of concerts when she's being so embarrassing. Plus she keeps pushing herself onto TV and once she wore a white tuxedo on a record sleeve and she had her hair dyed black even though in reality her real hair colour is as light as mine. But on the record sleeve she had it dyed all black, and she sat on stage wearing a white tuxedo.

Nobody else's sister would ever have that sort of picture taken.

And that's very embarrassing.

Once I tried to listen to one of her records, but it wasn't a record for people, it was the sort of music you can't listen to because it's not even music. I have no idea who buys music like that. And Ivana was sitting on a stage, and not even at the piano.

Because that's what she's like.

A stage is where people perform for other people who watch them. It doesn't always have to be on the piano. Once I performed on stage at the Cultural Centre, too It was when I was picked to recite the Young Pioneer's Oath. Everyone clapped and drummers drummed their drums and trumpeters played their trumpets. The trumpets had Young Pioneers' Flags hanging from them. The flags were golden. They all had a fringe. The fringes were golden, too The Young Pioneers' Flags had all sorts of things embroidered on them but I forget what was embroidered on them, because that wasn't what was very important. What was very important was me due to reciting the Young Pioneer's Oath.

In my class there were all sorts of good students and pupils, both boys and girls and whatever, and everyone wanted to recite the Young Pioneer's Oath but it wasn't them the High Ups picked, they picked me because everyone respected me even back then due to waste paper, and it was due to waste paper that I got the book called *The Young Pioneer's Heart* and made friends with Karol Gunár (PhD Social Sciences).

I'm sure that otherwise they would have picked Darinka Gunárová to recite the Young Pioneer's Oath on behalf of our class because she was top of the class, but they didn't pick her because it would have looked weird if Darinka had been reciting the Young Pioneer's Oath and her father would have been standing on stage with the other High Ups tying our Young Pioneers' Scarves, so that's why they didn't pick her and they picked me instead.

I was so good at reciting the Young Pioneer's Oath that afterwards all the people said I was the best at reciting it. And they said that nobody had ever been so good at reciting the Young Pioneer's Oath as I was. Everybody said so, including Grandaddy, and he also said that I did really well reciting the Oath and that's why we all went to a café.

Another thing that people said afterwards was that I was really good at saluting. I was so good at saluting that I even showed other children who were not so good at it how to salute. I am still very good at saluting but it's not the done thing any more because Young Pioneers have been abolished along with Young Pioneer Leaders. Young Pioneer Leaders were the people who used to lead the Young Pioneers. We used to have a Young Pioneers' Club too and we used to go there to play all sorts of games that were interesting and fun. I forget what sort of games we used to play there. But they were very interesting. Anyway.

Originally it was my Dad who was supposed to come along regarding the Young Pioneer's Oath but he didn't want to come and said that he had to look after my Mum regarding her bad back but I know that he wasn't really looking after her back and that it was just an excuse, because he made fun of it and didn't take the Young Pioneer's Oath seriously.

But on the other hand it was quite handy because my Dad would have never invited Karol Gunár (PhD Social Sciences) to the café because he was economical and never went to cafés.

Grandaddy was also economical but he did invite Karol Gunár (PhD Social Sciences) anyway, because he respected him very much due to his modesty and due to being humorous regarding funny jokes. Every time he said a funny joke Grandaddy laughed for a long time. Sometimes I almost thought he would never stop laughing. And when he was done this is what he always said:

'That was a good one!'

Meaning it was a really good one.

Karol Gunár (PhD Social Sciences) was very fond of Grandaddy, too That's why he always told him funny jokes.

And then we drank some yellow fizzy drink.

We used to have other kinds of fizzy drinks in the old days too, for example a red fizzy drink, but yellow fizzy drink was my favourite although I liked the red one, too But yellow fizzy was my favourite.

Sometimes, Karol Gunár (PhD Social Sciences) said something that didn't make Grandaddy say 'That was a good one', but instead he laughed for a long time and then this was what he said:

'Oh you are naughty!'

And after that Gunár Karol (PhD Social Sciences) also laughed for a long time and he was very happy. Because he was naughty.

Grandaddy used to call him naughty mainly when they talked about Tonko Szedílek's Mum, the one that people called Katuša. And after that

Karol Gunár (PhD Social Sciences) told all sorts of funny stories but they would send me and Darinka Gunárová outside to get some air.

I have no idea why we had to go outside to get some air, because there was plenty of air in the café too, because if there hadn't been any air inside they wouldn't have been able to stay there either, and that's why sometimes I think that Grandaddy just said that we should go out to get some air but he didn't actually mean it. Sometimes I think that they just wanted to be alone and talk about Communist things because that's what they were both like and these things always had to be a big secret.

Yesterday I saw Darinka Gunárová outside the Cultural Centre. And she was wearing a black T-shirt on top of that short skirt. The T-shirt was all black and it wasn't very long at all because it was very short. It was so short that it didn't even reach her belt. And her belly button was showing. I didn't want to look that way because I've got I.Q. and I don't see why I should be looking at Darinka Gunárová's belly button, but what I don't get is why she couldn't buy a longer T-shirt, because it was very weird the way her belly button was showing in that T-shirt. And that's not done. I don't mean that a belly button is not done, what I mean is that it's not done to show it.

Because it's not done.

Anyway.

My Mum had never worn the sort of things that would have showed her belly button and neither would Margita, but then she's fat. Not even Ivana wears things like that, even though Ivana is like that and she always does things that are embarrassing.

So I'm sometimes embarrassed due to her.

Margita never does things that are embarrassing so I don't have to be embarrassed due to her, because she isn't like Ivana at all. Because Ivana is a great artist from Bratislava.

There's just one thing I'll never get and that's why great artists from Bratislava have to be so embarrassing.

Sometimes Alf Névéry could have been quite an embarrassment to me too, but he wasn't, because he never went out and he just took showers all the time. And he had no TV. But nobody knew about it so it wasn't embarrassing.

And that's why it wasn't embarrassing for me either.

I never do things that are embarrassing because I always know what's what and why and how. Even when I shout at people in the street I only shout back at them if they have shouted at me, otherwise I never shout at people. Because I know exactly what's what and why and how.

And regarding that I never wear T-shirts that show my belly button because it would get people talking.

People in Komárno used to say all sorts of things about Tonko's Mum Katuša Szedíleková, like what she was like and what she had been up to before she got out of bedlock, and they used to say that her problem used not to be regarding superstitious prejudices and religious things back then, it used to be regarding men and sexual things, but then her son Tonko was born out of bedlock because he was her son, and then they were both superstitious and religious, and they were both out of bedlock.

Once there was this woman in Komárno who was out of bedlock too, and her name was Fertigová. She and her daughter were both out of bedlock because she hated men and that's why she never got married even after her daughter was born. And when her daughter grew up she turned out just like her mother and also hated men, and then she got out of bedlock too because she also had a daughter and didn't get married.

So then there were three women called Fertigová and people used to call them the Three Fertigová Women and they used to say all sorts of things about them. But they didn't care due to hating all men.

But then another woman came along whose name was Dadáková and she said that her son was going to sue Fertigová № 2. because Fertigová № 3 was his daughter, so he had the right to sue her. So he went to court to sue her and the court said that he was the father of Fertigová № 3. That made him a winner and the court allowed him to pay money for Fertigová № 3.

After that Dadák kept paying money but none of the Fertigová Women respected him for that, they just made fun of him because they hated men.

So then Dadák became a loner due to being made fun of and he was so sad and unhappy that his mother decided to do something about it because she was very upset that he had turned out like that due to being made fun of. She was upset that the Fertigová Women were making fun of him even though they were all out of bedlock and he wasn't.

So then Dadáková went to see old Gusto Rúhe and told him that she would give him a whole pig if he put a spell on Fertigová № 2 just like he did on Erik Rak.

When I've finished writing this I will write about how old Gusto Rúhe had put a spell on Erik Rak because I've forgotten to write about it again.

But old Gusto Rúhe said that he would only put a spell on Fertigová № 2 if Dadáková let him grope her, and Dadáková got so worked up that she was struck by a stroke when she got back home because she was already quite old and she was offended regarding all that.

Then she got buried and had a funeral due to that but nobody felt sorry for her because everyone knew that she wanted to put a spell on Fertigová № 2 and people said that the biter got bitten.

I said so, too.

Because it was very instructive.

After that nobody talked to Dadák because nobody wanted to talk to him any more, and then Dadák hanged himself in the sty, next to the pig that Dadáková was going to give old Gusto Rúhe.

When he got buried due to the hanging the Three Fertigová Women came to the funeral, but they didn't cry at all.

I didn't cry at all either.

His name was Eugen Dadák and his Mum's name was Elvíra Dadáková.

I knew Eugen Dadák very well because he was my Mum's last pupil regarding the piano, because he wanted to be educated even though he was already grown up. My Mum always used to say that Eugen Dadák had a feeling for the piano.

My Mum could always tell who had a feeling for the piano, for example she always used to say that Darinka Gunárová had a great feeling for the piano and what a great pity it was that she had given it up. Darinka Gunárová gave it up when her arms got like that after all those things happened, and she gave up the piano and stopped coming to our house regarding the piano.

Because my Mum always had a feeling about who had a feeling, because my Mum could have become a great artist herself regarding the piano, except that she got ill with a bad back and never became a great artist.

When my Mum was still a little girl because she was only four years old, she was already such a great artist that she was once asked to play for President Masaryk.

President Masaryk was a President way back when we still had Czechoslovakia, so we had a Czechoslovak President, too But he wasn't a Working Class President, he was a Capitalist one.

My Mum used to play the piano in Topoľčianky which is a resort where all the Presidents used to go. She wore a white dress. Grandmummy and Grandaddy and Uncle Otto went with her. And then my Mum was given a signed photograph along with a little statue. It was a statue of a girl with geese. The girl and the geese were all made out of china. My Mum had so much respect for them that she kept them in a glass case all her life.

The photo showed President Masaryk but I've never seen him, because after the Capitalists were gone and the Communist Party came, Grandaddy took the photograph away and burned it. Because it showed President Masaryk and he was a Capitalist and you never know what might happen.

That made my Mum very sad and she used to say that Grandaddy shouldn't have done that to her.

But Grandaddy did it because you can't be too careful.

My Mum loved President Masaryk and so did my Dad, even though he was a Czech. But my Dad hated the First Working Class President Klement Gottwald and this is how he used to make fun of him:

'Little Klement
Big excrement.'

Meaning he was being rude, because excrement is a rude word.

I really hated it when my Dad said rude things about the First Working Class President Klement Gottwald because I was frightened that Karol Gunár (PhD Social Sciences) might find out about it, because he loved him due to the Persian hat and due to having the same initials. I was frightened that he might find out about the sort of things my Dad had said about the First Working Class President and that he might be offended, so instead I went and reported it. Because you never know what might happen and what's what and why and how, right?

Right.

Karol Gunár (PhD Social Sciences) was very pleased that I told him.

We were both very pleased after I told him.

Every time I went to see Karol Gunár (PhD Social Sciences) in the Communist Party I was very pleased, because not everyone was allowed to go in there whenever they felt like it. The only people who could go in there were those who were allowed to go in there. And I was always allowed to go in there. There was a big staircase with a security man at the entrance. The security man wore a uniform. All the security men knew me and they always said, 'Hello Samko, here you are again,' and they would ring up to Karol Gunár (PhD Social Sciences) to ask if I could go up to see him without me having to ask them, because you couldn't just go and see him just like that.

It wasn't just like that at all.

He had a secretary as well as walls made of wood. It was very nice.

Other people, like my Dad or my Mum, were never in the Communist Party, only me and Grandaddy but he's only been to the Ground Floor. That's why people envied me because I used to go into the Communist Party whenever I felt like it. This is what it said on the door of Karol Gunár's (PhD Social Sciences)'s office:

Karol Gunár (PhD Social Sciences).
Secretary

Sometimes I had to wait too because everybody there was very hard-working and sometimes they worked very hard. Then I would look out of the window and I could see the Water Tower. Every time I waited for Karol Gunár (PhD Social Sciences) I looked at the Water Tower.

It was very tall.

Later they built a fence around it. They built the fence around it after it all happened to Tonko Szedílek. The fence was very tall, too.

I myself am not very tall but that's only because of this illness that I have, otherwise I'm healthy and hard-working. And I'm respected by people and everybody else.

Anyway.

There's just one thing I don't get and that's why Tonko said that he didn't care what Darinka Gunárová did, but sometimes he looked at her in a funny way and then I didn't know what was what and why and how, because of the way he looked at her. And she also looked at him like that but then all the girls looked at him like that because he was very well developed regarding P.E. and all the girls used to notice him due to that.

I didn't notice him like that because I'm not a girl.

But Tonko said that he didn't care about Darinka Gunárová, even though she had lots of white teeth and even though she came top of our class regarding schoolwork.

Sometimes Tonko told me what it was like Up There and how every-one loved one another and he also told me about his Father who was Up There and how his Father would come and get him one day and how he would take me along and everything would be all right then. He never said that Darinka Gunárová was supposed to go Up There too because he always said that he wasn't interested in Darinka Gunárová.

That's why I thought that it was very weird when I found out that Darinka Gunárová was supposed to go up the Water Tower, too.

Because that had always been our big secret, all these things regarding his Father and what it was like Up There and that's why I never told anyone, not even Karol Gunár (PhD Social Sciences), because I didn't know if I was supposed to report regarding Tonko as well. Sometimes I reported things regarding Katuša Szedíleková because we used to go and see her at work sometimes. She had a job regarding the Sewers and other kinds of water. That's what Katuša Szedíleková did. And Tonko and I would sometimes go and see her and sometimes we were allowed to stamp things.

Katuša Szedíleková had all sorts of rubber stamps. I used to love stamping things because I liked it very much. Sometimes she would let me stamp envelopes. I loved doing that, too.

Nobody in my family had a rubber stamp and I wasn't very happy about that because I love stamping things. My Dad's job was regarding woodworking and they didn't have any rubber stamps there, and my Mum had a disabled back so she didn't have any rubber stamps either, and neither did Grandaddy even though he had his Notebook which was very important even though its pages weren't lined.

But these days anyone can have a rubber stamp, even that idiot Krkan from Recycling has one but I'm never going to ask him to let me stamp things because I don't want that idiot Krkan to think he and his Recycling are something special.

Ivana and Žebrák don't have any rubber stamps either because artists don't have rubber stamps. Margita is the only one who has some due to sending children to children's homes because it's the law to have rubber stamps when you do that.

Except that Margita doesn't like me to come and see her at work and that's why I've never been to see her at work, so I can't ask her to let me stamp envelopes because I never go to see her at work.

Sometimes when I have lunch at her house Margita tells these stories about how she sent a child into a children's home and what it was like and whatever and sometimes when she tells a story like that I think to myself that I'm really good at stamping envelopes and that sending children into children's homes is not such a big deal either, so Margita can keep all those stories to herself.

But Margita knows everyone in Komárno due to her work and everyone knows her and all the Gypsies are scared of her and say hello to her.

I'm not scared of her because I'm not a Gypsy.

When Margita was little my Mum wanted her to play the piano too but she saw that Margita's feeling for the piano wasn't as good as Ivana's and she didn't make Margita play any more. Only sometimes. My Mum has never made me play the piano even though we had a piano at home all the time so I could have played any time but I never did because I wasn't good at it.

My Dad wasn't good at playing the piano either, but he was very good at tying knots. He had a book on knot tying and when he was in the mood he got me to play this game where I held the book and picked a word, for example Fisherman and my Dad would tie the Fisherman's Knot. Or the Round Knot. My Dad knew how to tie all the knots in the book but I didn't think this game was much fun because it wasn't fun at all.

But he taught me how to tie all sorts of knots anyway and that's come in very handy because when I load my handcart with cardboard, I have to tie it all up so it doesn't fall off because it often falls off and that's why it's very handy knowing how to tie all sorts of knots, for example the Round Knot.

The Round Knot is really good and it never comes undone.

But Žebrák, for example, wasn't so good at tying knots and when my Dad asked him to hold his book and test him regarding all the knots Žebrák made a funny face, so in the end my Dad told him to forget about it and later he said that Žebrák was a loser who couldn't even tie his own shoelaces, let alone a Round Knot.

Sometimes when my Dad was in the mood he also asked the children at school to test him regarding the knots in his book.

The book had a title that went like this:

A Hundred and One Ways to Tie a Knot

My Dad knew how to tie all the knots in the book and that was very handy. Anyway.

When my Grandfather from Detva came to visit he always used to tell my Dad how everyone in Detva still remembered him and everyone said that ever since Emil had moved away there was nobody left in Detva who could tie knots like that any more.

And that made my Dad very happy.

It made me very happy, too.

Another person in my family who was good at tying knots was Uncle Otto but he never asked us to test him regarding tying knots because he had a Mission regarding mushrooms but that was due to the lightning so people used to forgive him all sorts of things, even though they sometimes looked at him in a funny way because he used to do the sort of things nobody else in Komárno did.

For example, he used to talk to mushrooms.

It was very weird.

Once he took me to a forest, even though there are no forests in Komárno, but Uncle Otto found one with mushrooms growing in a circle. I'm not making it up, there really were mushrooms growing in this circle and in the middle of the circle there were no mushrooms.

And when we got there he stood in the middle of the circle and this is what he said as he stood there:

'This is Samko Tále from Komárno.'

I thought it was very weird that he was introducing me to mushrooms because I've never met anyone who would talk to mushrooms, except my Dad sometimes talked to the radio, but nobody in the whole world or even on TV has ever talked to mushrooms.

That's why I thought it was very weird.

Then Uncle Otto said that this circle was mine and that I would always find mushrooms there but I've never been back to that place because I can't remember where it was.

And when he was standing in the circle he told me that every person in the world had their circle like that and once you found your own circle you could make miracles happen regarding your body and soul due to these mushrooms. Then he told me that his own circle was in Balakhashka, the village where the lightning struck him in the shoulder and went out of his foot while he was in a caravan in the Soviet Union.

Uncle Otto said that the most important thing that happened when he returned to his body and to the other radio operators was that he discovered that the caravan stood right in the middle of one of those mushroom circles and that's why Uncle Otto believed that it was this circle that had sucked in the lightning and that was why it didn't stay in his shoulder but went out of his foot and he was saved due to that, except that afterwards he had a Mission.

And sometimes Uncle Otto used to say that he had only borrowed it from the mushrooms and that one day he would have to give it back to the mushrooms.

I have no idea what he meant by giving it back because I think it's rubbish to say that you have to give something back to mushrooms, because I've never heard of anyone borrowing anything from mushrooms because it's out of the question, even though Uncle Otto was really weird and people never argued with him about it because they thought that it was very weird.

Because he was really very weird.

But then again, sometimes I think it's quite handy that I can't remember where my mushroom circle is because I've never borrowed anything from it but you never know what might happen and what's what and why and how. And I'm no retard, so why should I borrow anything from a mushroom circle that I would have to give back later, right?

Right.

Because I never borrow anything from anyone because I can look after myself and that's why I don't need to borrow anything from anyone.

Because that's out of the question.

Uncle Otto was also weird regarding telling everyone that he knew how to cure mankind regarding a nuclear bomb explosion.

Uncle Otto used to say that mankind could be cured regarding a nuclear explosion by growing Siberian Woodrot.

Siberian Woodrot was a kind of mushroom that didn't grow in the ground, it grew on wood, like nails. Uncle Otto used to say that Siberian Woodrot had lots of good qualities that could save mankind from disaster if people grew Siberian Woodrot in their homes because it could swallow nuclear fumes.

And he also used to say that Siberian Woodrot could be spun into a yarn which could be used for making clothes and if all mankind wore clothes made out of Siberian Woodrot we could all be saved regarding a nuclear bomb explosion.

Because in those days everyone was frightened regarding a nuclear bomb explosion, because that was the law. Nowadays people are not so frightened regarding a nuclear bomb explosion because they are frightened regarding other frightening things. But back then a nuclear explosion was the most frightening thing of all.

Once there was this woman in Komárno whose name was Auntie Husličková and she used to live in one of those old tenement houses behind the cemetery and she believed that the best thing for a nuclear bomb explosion was mustard because if you covered yourself in mustard you would be saved regarding an explosion.

That's why she kept buying mustard and she ended up with so much mustard that her larder was full of it and she had to have special shelves built in the hallway and in the cellar and all over her flat. She had shelves with mustard all over the place.

Then one day she died and they didn't find her for three weeks. They found her in the hallway, by the smell that was coming from the hallway which meant she was really lucky that she died in the hallway because if she had died in her living room it would have been even longer before she was found.

Auntie Husličková didn't have any relatives anywhere except for some neighbours, so they had to clear out her flat and they had to take all the mustard to the skip to clear it out. The pile of mustard was really big, as big as the whole skip. But hardly anyone wanted to have any of it, not even the Gypsies.

And then they found a list of names called 'Not To Be Given Mustard' in Auntie Husličková's prayer book. Auntie Husličková had it at hand so that if an explosion happened she would know straight away who should be saved and who shouldn't. Lots of names on the list were crossed out and then added again. Some were underlined in red pencil.

Auntie Husličková was buried for free with state money because she didn't leave any money, due to buying all that mustard.

There were only two people at her funeral and now you can't even see where her grave is because it's all overgrown and due to that it's invisible.

Her name was Božena Husličková.

I love mustard, especially with sausages. I love sausages. Sometimes I can eat even four. Sometimes I eat only three. Sometimes I have sausages for breakfast. Sometimes I eat only two. Sausages with mustard are the best.

Anyway.

Uncle Otto wrote a letter to the High Ups telling them about Siberian Woodrot and how important it was and how it should be grown and spun into a yarn but he never got a reply because the High Ups knew all about Uncle Otto and his disability regarding his nerves, so they never replied even though he even wrote letters to Presidents. Sometimes he sat in the kitchen crying and wondering how he was supposed to save mankind if people didn't want to grow Siberian Woodrot.

And after that he drew a picture on the back of a plastic tablecloth in the kitchen. The picture was called *The Safe City* and it was drawn in ink pencil. The picture showed a city with a big roof above that covered the whole city and there was Siberian Woodrot growing all over the roof. Uncle Otto said that even if an explosion happened right above the roof, the city would be safe and out of harm's way.

But the greatest problem with Siberian Woodrot was that it always used to stink after rain. Even though he grew Siberian Woodrot inside our flat it always knew when it rained outside, and then it stank. It stank like rotten potatoes. That's what Siberian Woodrot stank like after rain. Like rotten potatoes.

Sometimes I think that mankind didn't want to grow it because it stank so bad. Like rotten potatoes.

And then Uncle Otto wrote to America regarding Siberian Woodrot because he never got a reply from anyone here, but instead of getting a reply from America he was summoned to the police and told to stop writing letters or he'd get into big trouble.

But Uncle Otto didn't stop, because he believed that he had a Mission which meant that he could write letters to America and whatever, and then Grandaddy got so frightened that he locked him up at home to stop him sending letters. But sometimes at night Uncle Otto ran away because he needed mushrooms. And when he came back he brought mushrooms wrapped in newspaper and he was all dirty due to sleeping in the woods.

And that was very embarrassing for Grandaddy.

It was very embarrassing for me, too.

When Alf Névéry moved into Uncle Otto's old flat he hung the plastic tablecloth on the wall like a picture and watched it instead of TV and drank alcoholic drinks as he sat watching it.

Then he died and Ivana took the plastic tablecloth and said that she would keep it.

She can keep it for all I care. Perhaps she thinks that I need it but I don't need it, so there, she can keep it because I've got lots of tablecloths of my own and I don't need to hang them on my wall or anywhere else, because I have lots of lovely pictures hanging there that I bought with my own hands and brought back on my own handcart because I've got three of them. They are really lovely. They have lovely frames, too One of the pictures is called *Springtime on the Plains* and it shows springtime on the plains. The second one is called *Summertime on the Plains* and it shows summertime on the plains. The third one is called *Wintertime on the Plains* and it shows wintertime on the plains. I didn't buy *Autumn on the Plains* because they didn't have it, but that's very handy because there's a door that opens to the balcony on my fourth wall so I don't need a picture there.

The pictures are in gold frames. Sometimes I have to dust them. I don't know what else I could say about the pictures.

Sometimes when I watch TV but I'm not really watching because it's not very interesting, like when they are just talking, I watch *Summertime on the Plains* because it's right above the TV.

Summertime on the Plains is beautiful.

But soap operas are the best. I love soap operas best of all. Soap operas are very good and lovely. The best thing about them is that they always start on time. What I like about soap operas is that they always start at the same time. That's what I love most about soap operas.

Everyone in the world loves soap operas.

I love soap operas, too.

Anyway.

Except for Ivana because she hates soap operas and I can't stand it when Ivana is like that and when she makes fun of soap operas and says nasty things about them. But the one thing I don't get is what is it that she likes if she doesn't like soap operas. Because everyone likes soap operas, right?

Right.

Margita, for example, loves soap operas even though she sometimes laughs at herself for watching them. Valent Anka sometimes watches soap operas too, even though he sometimes laughs at himself for watching them. Usually he watches sport.

I don't watch sport very much because I don't know any of these sportsmen, and that's why I don't watch them very much because I don't know who is who and I can't tell them apart. Valent Anka can always tell them apart. He always knows exactly who's who and from what team and he never gets it wrong.

That's very handy.

I like watching Slovak sportsmen best because I can tell them apart because they are Slovak.

And I support them, too I always wait for them to say on TV how the referee was unfair to our sportsmen again. When they say this on TV everyone gets very cross due to that.

I get cross, too.

Anyway.

The only thing I don't get is why I've got to write about the Cemetery. I have no idea what I'm supposed to write in the Cemetery Book because nobody told me. I really don't know why it's got to be about the Cemetery because there are so many other lovely places in Komárno that I could write about, like the Market Place. It would be really easy for me to write a Market Place Book if that was what it said in my fortune-telling, but the thing is old Gusto Rúhe's fortune-telling said that it I've got to write about the Cemetery and that's something I'll never get and I have no idea why it's got to be about the Cemetery because you can't write a good book about the Cemetery.

It's out of the question.

I know this because I've already tried once when I wrote my First Cemetery Book, the one that was only short but I still don't know if it counts as a Cemetery Book because I never got a reply and sometimes I think that they don't have any idea about what a proper Cemetery Book should be like.

Nobody in the whole world could write a Cemetery Book, not even Alf Névéry or Cyril Malacký. And that's why I don't get it why it has to be me who's got to write the Cemetery Book.

Once I asked this man whose name is Henrich Vigétz and he's a gravedigger and works at the Cemetery regarding grave digging, so I asked him what it's like at the Cemetery because I wanted to know what it's like and this is what he said:

'Bloody awful.'

But that's a rude word and I don't know if you're allowed to write words like that in books, even though Alf Névéry told me about a book by this man Miller from America that had even ruder words in it but he was from America and they can do whatever they feel like in America, but I don't know if you're allowed to write swearing words like that here in Slovakia.

I don't need to swear or use rude words because I never swear and if I swear it's only at people who shout at me or at Gypsies and queers or that idiot Krkan from Recycling. Because he doesn't take it from me but he does take it from that nasty rat-woman Angelika Édesová, and that's why I swear at him.

Once there was this man in Komárno but he wasn't from Komárno, he was from Dolný Kubín which is another city in Slovakia, and he used to swear like nobody had ever sworn before and his name was Tetrovec.

When I was very young and he was already very old, whenever he saw me with waste paper he always shouted that I was stealing his paper, because back then you could only collect waste paper, because there wasn't any cardboard around. Tetrovec wanted to beat me up for stealing his paper because he thought that all the waste paper in Komárno was his and that's why he thought that I wasn't allowed to collect waste paper.

But my Dad said that I shouldn't be scared of Tetrovec because he just shouted but he never did anything. So I wasn't scared of him. Because he just shouted and never did anything.

When he still lived in Dolný Kubín, Tetrovec used to get really mad whenever someone sat down. And he would tell them off and nobody in his family was allowed to sit down due to that, not even during meals or at any other time because it made Tetrovec really mad. Meaning they had to eat their meals standing round the table, because if Tetrovec saw them sitting down he said that he would beat them up with a whip, because he used to be very well-off regarding cattle to start with.

There were lots of chairs all over his house but nobody was allowed to sit on them. So they never sat on chairs, and then first all his sons moved out and then all his daughters moved out, then his wife died. And after that he lost all his property due to Nationalisation of all Property.

And then Tetrovec got even worse and every time he saw someone sitting down he would swear and tell them off for sitting down even if they were total strangers.

So they sent him to Komárno, because back then lots of Slovaks were sent to Komárno to make sure that lots of Slovaks would live there.

At first he worked in the State Wineries but everybody hated him there because he got into an argument with everyone, even the manager, regarding sitting down. And then he retired and started to collect waste paper.

Tetrovec never sat down and he lived until he was 92 years old, because that's when he died. And the way he died was that he slipped on the ice along with his handcart and broke his pelvis. The pelvis is a bone down there. You know where I mean. In the bottom.

Then he had to have an operation and the doctors said that he would never be able to sit properly, and when Tetrovec heard that he got so mad that he died.

His name was Jozef Tetrovec.

He used to stuff his ears with cotton wool and swear a lot.

There were some other people in Komárno who used to shout at me even though they didn't have cotton wool in their ears or collect waste paper, for example Stanislav Manica.

But he is a fat slob now.

There's just one thing I'd like to see, and that's Manica trying to squeeze into his Young Pioneer's Uniform. My Young Pioneer's Uniform still fits me so well that I could wear it any time. If they announced that a Young Pioneer's Oath was being taken in the Cultural Centre, I'd like to see who else could still go there and take the Young Pioneer's Oath regarding fitting into their Young Pioneer's Uniform.

But I could take the Oath as many times as I wanted to because I haven't turned into a fat slob due to my healthy life of style and plenty of exercise in the fresh air. And another reason I haven't turned into a fat slob is due to yoghurt. Because yoghurt is very good for you.

Anyway.

Nobody could take the Young Pioneer's Oath, except for me and Darinka Gunárová, because she hasn't turned into a fat slob either.

Yesterday I saw Darinka Gunárová outside the Cultural Centre. I was so surprised to see her regarding the golden footwear and the short T-shirt and her belly button showing that I didn't know what to say until Darinka Gunárová said this:

'How are you Samko?'

Meaning how I was.

And this is what I said:

'I'm fine.'

Meaning I was fine.

Because I take good care of myself and that's why I'm fine. And that's why I've got I.Q. and I'm very popular as well as very hard-working. And people respect me due to being hard-working.

When I'm out and about with my handcart sometimes as many as thirty people say hello to me because that's how well they know me. Some people know me due to deliveries I have made for them with my handcart. All the people I know are in my Surnames and Christian Names Notebooks. And when someone dies I always check if I've got them in my Surnames and Christian Names Notebooks because if I've got them there, it goes without saying that I can't have them in my Notebook called Died, too, right?

Right.

It's people like Uncle Otto who are the greatest problem regarding my Notebook called Died, because I don't know if their names should be there or not.

I've got a name under each letter in my Surnames notebook. I used not to have any names starting with the letter Q, but then luckily I met Darinka's husband the black man whose name is Samuel Quentin and that relieved me because it meant that now I have someone starting with a Q.

The thing is, there aren't any other people starting with the letter Q in Komárno. There's just this Pub called The Queen but that's not a person. But apart from that there isn't anyone starting with a Q.

Lots of names start with the letter H. And also with the letter S.

I don't know what else I could write regarding letters.

Sometimes I'm happy that Darinka's husband starts with the letter Q because that has made me complete.

But then again, sometimes I think that she shouldn't have married a black husband just because of that. And now she has two children with her husband the black man and both children are black as well. Her black children were at the funeral, too They've got curly hair. Their names are Anthony and Antony. Anthony is a boy and Antony is a girl.

And that's very weird.

I don't know how they can tell them apart with same names and same curly hair. And with both being black. Margita also has two sons but they are easy to tell apart because they aren't black. Their names are Patrik and Richard.

Ivana has three daughters and their names are Dorota, Dominika and Dita. That's very handy too because it's easy to remember due to all of them starting with the letter *D*. Dita is the only one that was difficult to remember because I haven't met anyone else with a name like that in Komárno or on TV. But that's just like Ivana, she's got to have at least one name that doesn't exist, because she's a great artist from Bratislava.

All three daughters have the surname Žebráková, only Ivana is called Ivana Tále. That's what it says on all the records and on TV. And her name doesn't end in *-ová*, as if she was a sort of a man called Ivana Tále.

But it goes without saying that if you're an artist you don't want to be called Žebráková on a record because it means beggar in Czech, right?

Right.

But Tále is a really lovely name and it's my surname, too But the worst thing is that people make my name rhyme with that rhyme about stinking. If it weren't for that rhyme about stinking I would love my name even more.

Everyone in my family is called Tále but apart from my family I don't know anyone else called Tále.

Once I saw this man on TV and when his name came up this is what it was: Ernest Tálle. But his name was spelled with 2 *L*s. My name is spelled with only one *L*. Like this: Tále.

And this Tálle's job was stuffing animals and he was from Žilina but he was spelled with 2 *L*s. And the other thing I didn't like about him was that he stuffed animals, even though I don't know him at all and I don't want to say anything bad about him, or ask him to stop stuffing animals but I don't like that because it stinks.

The reason I know it stinks is because we once had a stuffed fox at school and it really stank. It stank like a dog.

And that's why it's very weird that there are people who don't mind doing such stinky work. And that they are called Tálle, too That might make people think that we also stink because our name is Tále. Even though we're spelled with only one *L*.

But people don't think so because they respect us. And they especially respect me because I'm hard-working.

Because I've always been the most hard-working person in my family. Ivana has always been the least hard-working one, because all she's ever done is play the piano so that she wouldn't have to do any real work, for example take out the rubbish.

Margita has always been more hard-working because she used to do knitting and all sorts of other handiwork. Once she embroidered a Slovak crest on her son Patrik's tracksuit jacket before he went to America because you couldn't buy it in the shops and she wanted everyone in America to see straight away that Patrik had a Slovak crest embroidered on his tracksuit jacket.

It was lovely.

It had everything a crest is supposed to have, as well as a silver frame. Everyone praised Margita for embroidering such a beautiful Slovak crest.

I praised her, too.

Ivana would never embroider a Slovak crest onto a tracksuit jacket or onto anything else because that's what she's like and she won't even put a sticker with the Slovak crest on her car.

I do have a crest sticker on my handcart because I'm a road user and that's the law. I also have another crest on my handcart, it's the crest of the Vitana Food Company but that's not the law, it's just something I found on a cardboard box and I stuck it on because I felt like it. I also used to have a rude drawing on my handcart because it was drawn on by this man Ferdinand Mica who looks like a Gypsy, although he's not a Gypsy, and it was a very rude drawing of a word that you only say when you're swearing. He did it while I was away buying some Poprad Wafers because they are very tasty. So I got really worked up because Ferdinand Mica is dirty and he doesn't have a job because he gets money for not working, and I went and reported him to Karol Gunár (PhD Social Sciences) so that he knew what he'd drawn on my handcart and could make sure he'd get into big trouble.

Because it's forbidden to draw things like that on my handcart.

But Karol Gunár (PhD Social Sciences) said there was nothing he could do about Ferdinand Mica, because we got what we wanted and this was Democracy. And this is what we wanted.

But this is not what I wanted and I told Karol Gunár (PhD Social Sciences) many times repeatedly that nobody in the whole world or in Slovakia wanted it except for Ivana and Žebrák, because everyone else loved the Communist Party.

Because it was very nice.

And that's why everyone went to the May Day Parade because everyone loved the Communist Party and everyone wanted to wave to it.

I loved the May Day Parade best of all because it was the most beautiful thing in the world. Everyone was happy and waved to the High Ups who stood on the podium. Everyone held flags and all sorts of flapping things. Some people held a sort of flapping thing that was called the Flutterer. Flutterers were lovely and everyone loved flapping them.

I loved flapping them, too.

People were all very happy and they all shouted due to their happiness like this:

'Long live the Communist Party!'

Meaning the Communist party should live long.

You would never ever see so many people shouting regarding the Communist Party all year round as you did on May Day. Everyone was very happy.

I was very happy, too.

I always joined the parade and when I finished marching I went back to the podium and as the people marched by waving happily I always waved back to them happily.

Karol Gunár (PhD Social Sciences) was also always up there on the podium waving happily.

Only my Dad wasn't waving happily because he made fun of them. He used to say things like this:

'High and mighty on the stand,
On their arses they will land.'

But that was a very rude thing to say and I hated it when my Dad said things like that because Karol Gunár (PhD Social Sciences) wasn't like that at all because he was a PhD Social Sciences. And he and the other High Ups could stand on the podium for as long as they liked and they would never land anywhere.

And they always smiled happy smiles.

And when the May Day Parade was over you could buy oranges in the shops. Oranges were very special then, not like now when you can buy oranges whenever you feel like it. In those days you could only buy oranges on May Day so that everyone could see that we could afford oranges.

I don't actually like oranges very much, because they can be hard to peel sometimes. I prefer tangerines because they are easier to peel sometimes. But sometimes they have lots of pips so then I don't really like tangerines either.

Another thing that's bad about tangerines is that you're not supposed to drink yoghurt after eating them.

Because yoghurt is very good for you.

Anyway.

Sometimes I think that maybe I've been a writer for long enough and that it's impossible for anyone to write more than I have because it's out of the question that someone could be a writer more than I am. But then again, there are some books that are very thick but I haven't read them because I haven't got time for silly things such as reading thick books.

But the greatest problem is that I don't know what else I could write about the Cemetery. Why doesn't old Gusto Rúhe write his own Cemetery Book? But he is such an alcoholic that he doesn't even know how to write any more, and he's just showing off with that Moonstone of his regarding fortune-telling so that he can drink alcoholic drinks and grope women.

I would have stopped being a writer a long time ago but what he had written on the tarmac was: 'Will Write the Cemetery Book', which means that it's the law and if I don't write it I might get into big trouble because it's the law and I ought to write it because I'm not busy now, due to my handcart being in Ján Boš-Mojš's workshop.

Sometimes I think that I should have asked Alf Névéry how to write a Cemetery Book, but back then I didn't know that my rear-view mirror would break off, so I never asked him. Another person I could ask is Cyril Malacký because he's very helpful, and he once changed the glass on the door downstairs, but I'm sure he would ask why I'm asking and then he might tell everyone and then everyone would know and everyone would ask what I was writing about and everyone would want to read it. But I don't want everyone to ask me and to read it because then they could make fun of me.

And I hate it when people make fun of me.

Anyway.

Some people always used to make fun of Uncle Otto too regarding his Mission and because he wanted to cure everyone and because he kept giving everyone dried mushrooms.

But most of all they laughed at him due to a mushroom called the Gappy Goodwink. Because Uncle Otto said that if all mankind ate Gappy Goodwinks starting when they were little children then everyone in the whole world would be happy because Gappy Goodwink would bring happiness to all mankind.

Because that's what Gappy Goodwink could do.

But people didn't believe him and nobody wanted to eat Gappy Goodwinks, starting when they were little children, due to that.

I didn't eat them either.

But I'm very happy and very kind anyway even without eating Gappy Goodwinks. And you can tell that I'm like that due to my kindness and due to never making fun of other people. I only make fun of other people sometimes when they make fun of me, and if I didn't make fun of them they would think they could keep making fun of me. So that's why I make fun of them.

My Dad used to make fun of people all the time and I really hated that, because it was forbidden and it always got me very worked up. My Mum never made fun of people, but that was because she was busy or because her back was hurting or because she was giving piano lessons. Margita doesn't make fun of people either because she's kind-hearted. Ivana always makes fun of everyone but if she goes on like that she'll get reported regarding crying in the toilet. She shouldn't think that she can make fun of people just because she's a great artist from Bratislava.

Once there was this man in Komárno and everyone kept making fun of him because he didn't have a name because he wasn't normal due to being subnormal. And the way you could tell was because every morning he went to the River Danube which is a big river that runs through Komárno, and he collected driftwood that had floated down the Danube. Then he put it out to dry. And when it was dry he would hold it to his ear and knock it with a wooden hammer. Then he would listen for a long time to the sound the wood made regarding the hammer. If the sound was good he would say:

'Good wood.'

And he would throw the good wood back into the River Danube. If the sound it made wasn't good he would say:

'Bad wood.'

And he would throw the bad wood back into the River Danube, too.

That's why people made fun of him and they called him Good Wood because nobody knew what his name was because he never said anything except good wood or bad wood. He used to live on a rubbish dump behind the bridge.

Sometimes when people found the driftwood that he had put out to dry so that he could knock it with his hammer they threw it into the Danube and everyone looked forward to seeing Good Wood get all worked up when he couldn't find it.

I looked forward to it, too.

And he always got worked up and banged the ground with his wooden hammer and shouted all sorts of shouts because that was all he could do.

And then he was run over by a car because he wasn't paying attention due to knocking while he was standing in the middle of the road.

So that's how he died.

And after he died they found out from the Documents that he had a name which was Abbé Pierre. And that he was from Bratislava to start with.

And everyone thought it was really weird that he had such a foreign name and that he came from Bratislava, but was subnormal in Komárno.

I thought it was really weird, too.

Another weird thing about him was that he didn't have the sort of wrinkles like normal people have that go in a straight line from one side to the other. Instead his wrinkles went in a straight line from top to bottom. I've never seen anyone else with wrinkles on their forehead that went from top to bottom and not from one side to another. Everyone said it was very weird.

I said it was weird, too.

My Dad had wrinkles that were proper and so did my Grandfather from Detva. Grandaddy didn't have many wrinkles, just a wart on his ear. I don't have wrinkles either, because I'm still young and have a healthy life of style and I get plenty of exercise.

Especially in the fresh air.

Anyway.

Karol Gunár (PhD Social Sciences) had a wrinkle on his forehead that moved when he frowned. Nobody else in the world could frown and make their wrinkle move like that. It was so humorous that I always asked him to frown when he was in a humorous mood and then he made his wrinkle move. I always looked forward to him making his wrinkle move like that.

Because nobody else in the world could do this, only Karol Gunár (PhD Social Sciences).

Yesterday I saw Darinka Gunárová outside the Cultural Centre. And the most important thing was that she had butterflies on her head.

Honestly, I'm not making it up, because I'm no retard and I would never make up things like that, but she really had butterflies on her head and the butterflies were moving even though they weren't real.

I have never seen such a thing in my life, not in Komárno or anywhere else in the world, not even on TV. I've never ever seen anyone with butterflies on their head like Darinka Gunárová. I've seen all sorts of things on TV, for example people with lots of tattoos tattooed on their bodies but I've never seen anyone with butterflies on their head, not once.

Because we have tattoos in Komárno too, for example that rat-woman Angelika Édesová, who keeps stealing my cardboard from the Market Place, she has a tattoo on her arm that says 'I love Lali'. Meaning she loves Lali. And what she means is she loves Lali Fénšég who's a jailbird and a Gypsy. But it didn't help her because when Lali Fénšég came back from jail he didn't marry Angelika Édesová, he married her sister Claudia Édesová instead. Serves her right, that rat-woman Angelika Édesová.

After that she was sorry that she had this tattoo which said 'I love Lali' tattooed on her arm. So she asked him and her sister Claudia Édesová to come and watch and then she got an axe and tried to chop off her arm with the tattoo.

But she didn't manage to whack it hard enough and the axe just hit the bone but her arm stayed on and it's all crooked now and it makes everyone laugh.

It makes me laugh, too.

The only person who doesn't laugh at it is that idiot Krkan because that's what he's like and he will do sexual things with anyone, even Gypsies, and every time he does it he puts up a note that says 'Back Soon'. Except he's never back soon.

Even that nasty rat-woman Angelika Édesová doesn't have butterflies on her head, so it's out of the question that Darinka Gunárová should go around with butterflies on her head and I have no idea why she does it. I don't want Darinka Gunárová to go around like that. And that's why I didn't know what to say because what can you say to someone who goes around with butterflies fixed to their head. That's why I didn't say anything, but this is what Darinka Gunárová said then:

'Where are you going Samko?'

Meaning where I was going.

And this is what I said:
'I'm going this way.'
Meaning I was going this way.
And this is what Darinka Gunárová said then:
'I'm going to the Cemetery, would you like to come with me?'
Meaning she was going to the Cemetery, and would I like to come with her.

But the thing is I didn't quite know what to do because I couldn't really go to the Cemetery with Darinka Gunárová because we were standing in the One-Way Street behind the Cultural Centre and if I went to the Cemetery with Darinka Gunárová I would have had to turn round and go down a One-Way Street the wrong way and that could have been a total disaster regarding me being a road user because I have my handcart and it's the law for road users with handcarts.

Because it goes without saying that I'm a proper road user just like everyone else and if I had turned around and gone down a One-Way Street the wrong way with Darinka Gunárová people might have laughed at me due to not knowing what a One-Way Street was.

Because it's the law.

So I had no idea what to do because nobody told me what to do, and when that happens I get very worked up and I'm not supposed to get worked up regarding my state of health. So I didn't get worked up and instead this is what I said:

'In our good old Cemetery
A dead man hangs from every tree.'

Meaning it was very humorous.

Because my Grandfather from Detva knew lots of humorous sentences like this and he always used to say them whenever he heard someone say some word. And if people said one of those words for which he had a humorous sentence he would always say it. For example, when he heard the word Cemetery this is what he used to say:

'In our good old cemetery
A dead man hangs from every tree.'

Or when someone said the Hungarian greeting *kezét csókolom* this is what he always said:

'*Kezét csókolom*, how d'you do?
That's in Hungarian, so sod you!'

Or when he heard a bell ringing this is what he always said:

'Ding dang dong,
All Jews pong.'

That was always very humorous. And that's why I thought that Darinka Gunárová would laugh if I said:

'In our good old Cemetery
A dead man hangs from every tree.'

But she didn't laugh at all and instead she just shook her head a little and that made all the butterflies flap their wings.

It was very weird.

The one thing I'll never get is what those butterflies on her head were for. But I didn't want to ask why she was wearing a thing on her head like nobody else ever wears on their head so I didn't ask.

And after that this is what Darinka Gunárová said:

'I'll be off now.'

Meaning she would be off now.

And then I said:

'I'll be off, too'

Meaning I would be off, too.

And after that Darinka Gunárová left. So I left, too But I went down the One-Way Street the right way, because otherwise I would be in trouble due to being a road user.

Darinka Gunárová could go wherever she wanted because she's not a road user.

But I am a road user and that's why I get praised by everyone.

Because I always get lots of praise from everyone, including from Karol Gunár (PhD Social Sciences) because he has always praised me a lot, but he praised me most of all when that thing happened with Tonko Szedílek because I reported it to him. Then he patted me on the back and said that I was the best boy in Komárno because I'd told him everything.

The reason why I told him everything was because it was supposed to be me that was meant to go up the Water Tower with Tonko Szedílek to start with, because he always said that he would take me along when he went Up There on his fourteenth birthday and that he would show me how happy people were Up There because of their happy lives.

The thing is that the only way to get up the Water Tower was to climb up the lightning rod but Tonko said that we would manage because his Father would be there to help us. Of course, Tonko was very good at P.E. but I was excepted from P.E. and that's why I didn't know what was what and why and how.

I have no idea why we were supposed to climb up the Water Tower and why it was the law for him to go up there to meet his Father. Nobody ever told me why he had to go up there and all I knew was that it was meant to be on his birthday regarding being fourteen years old. Because Tonko's birthday was regarding being born.

I also have a birthday every year. Because it goes without saying that everyone in the world has their birthday every year. Even people who've died have their birthday every year.

Tonko's birthday always used to be on the first of September and the way you could tell was because it was the first day of school because school always started on the first of September. And that's how I always remembered.

My birthday is on the twelfth of November. That's a lovely date for a birthday. I'm very happy that I was born on the twelfth of November. And that's why my birthday is always on the twelfth of November.

My Mum used to buy lottery tickets all her life and she always picked the numbers regarding the birthdays of everyone in my family but she never won. She used to say that she had spent so much money on lottery tickets that if she got all that money back she could buy a car.

Except that she never got any money back, so we never had a car.

Even though we were very economical.

My Grandfather from Detva once said that there was this man in Detva who had won first prize in the lottery but then all sorts of bad things happened to him, so he became an alcoholic and got divorced. And then everyone was happy that all those bad things happened to him even though he had won first prize in the lottery. And everybody said it served him right.

I said it served him right, too.

I once won too but not in the lottery, but due to collecting waste paper and that was when I came top of the whole school because nobody else came more top than I did. And that's when I got *The Young Pioneer's Heart* and I was reported on the school radio because I came top.

That was very tiring because it wasn't easy to win at all. Because I was always very well prepared for collecting because I would go around all the shopkeepers in advance asking them to put their waste paper aside for me and not to give it to anyone else except me. So when the collection date was announced I would already be well prepared but nobody else would be prepared and due to that I always came top in the whole school.

Because I'm very hard-working.

Ivana once won the first prize too but it goes without saying that she didn't win due to collecting waste paper. The prize she won was regarding the piano. She won it in Hradec Králové. Hradec Králové is a Czech town. But that was when we still had Czechoslovakia so it was OK to win in Hradec Králové.

Then she got given all sorts of diplomas and medals and everyone said that she had a great feeling for the piano.

I said it, too.

But I'd like to see how Ivana would manage collecting cardboard anyway because all she is good at is the piano and she doesn't have the strength to push the handcart, not even for two steps, let alone all the way to Recycling. And another thing I'd like to see her do is argue with that idiot Krkan from Recycling about lying and not taking it when it's wet.

The thing is, I did report him to Karol Gunár (PhD Social Sciences) a long time ago, but all he said was that this was what we wanted, this was that Democracy of ours and now it was up to other people to sort out that idiot Krkan.

Because when we still had the Communist Party he could sort out everything because he was High Up and it was the law for them to sort everything out. And that's why he sorted out Darinka Gunárová too, because I told him. Because he said I should always report everything to him. So then I always told him everything, and another reason why I always told him everything was because he always knew what to do and I wanted him to tell me what to do.

On that First School Day when it all happened Karol Gunár (PhD Social Sciences) was also in our school because he loved children and he was very kind in all sorts of other ways, too And that's why he always got invited to the First School Day Assembly and he would stand on stage and say all sorts of things into the microphone.

Because that was the law for the High Ups.

The other children were not listening to what he was saying and some were misbehaving but I was listening because I was paying attention but then Darinka Gunárová and Tonko Szedílek distracted me when they told me that they were going up the Water Tower that night and that I shouldn't tell anyone. I wanted to ask when it would be my turn to go up the Water Tower but they weren't listening because they were just looking at each other and that's why they didn't listen to me.

So I didn't know what to do about it and I got very worked up.

So I went to see Karol Gunár (PhD Social Sciences) because the First School Day Assembly was over and that was very handy, and I told him that I had something to report. And he said I should tell him. So I told him everything about everything and about Darinka Gunárová.

After that Karol Gunár (PhD Social Sciences) went all red. He went so red that he was all red like the colour red. That's how red he got.

Then I got frightened that I would get the blame for telling it but I didn't get the blame, and instead I got praise for telling. I was very happy that I got praise for telling.

Then he said that I shouldn't think about it any more and that he would sort everything out.

So I stopped thinking about it.

And then I went home.

And then I got home.

And then I went to sleep.

And then I woke up because of this weird nice smell.

I have no idea where that smell came from because it was the kind of smell I had never smelled before, not even on TV, and that's why I was very surprised and I went to see my Mum in the kitchen and asked her about the smell but my Mum couldn't smell anything because she had lost her smell when she had her bad back cured so it goes without saying that she couldn't smell the weird smell either. She said that it must have been something I had dreamt and that I should go back to bed. So I went back to bed and then I went back to sleep.

And then I woke up because it was the morning and I went to the piano room and I saw that Karol Gunár (PhD Social Sciences) and Darinka Gunárová were in the piano room which was very weird, because they had never been in our house before except for Darinka Gunárová because she used to come to my Mum for piano lessons because she had a feeling for it.

And another weird thing was that it was in the morning because we usually never had visitors in the morning because that's not the time for visitors. Because it's the morning.

Darinka Gunárová was sitting on the piano stool looking at the piano but you could tell that in reality she wasn't really looking at the piano at all, she just looked like she was looking at it. And both her arms were bandaged all the way up to her elbows.

It was very weird.

And she put a little golliwog on the piano lid. A golliwog was a little doll that was all black and naked except for little rings it had in its ears regarding earrings. It was made of rubber.

And that's when Karol Gunár (PhD Social Sciences) told me about the tragic disaster that had happened because Tonko Szedílek had fallen off the Water Tower at night because he probably tried to climb up to the top by the lightning rod, and due to that he fell down and onto his head and he broke his head. And due to that he died.

I had no idea what to say to that because I didn't know. Then my Dad took me to the kitchen and he shouted at me in a low voice about why I hadn't told him anything and why he had to find out like this and if I ever told anyone that we had known about this and that Darinka Gunárová was also meant to go up there, I would end up in jail and so would Ivana and Margita and Mum and Dad and Karol Gunár (PhD Social Sciences), and especially Darinka Gunárová. He asked if that was what I wanted. And I said that it wasn't what I wanted.

Then my Dad said that nobody could have known that Tonko wanted to climb up the Water Tower. And that I should mark his words. And that he was born out of bedlock and due to that he wasn't right in the head. So it was his own business and we should be glad that things turned out the way they did.

So I was glad that things turned out the way they did.

But it was all very weird anyway.

Then I took off my pyjamas.

Then Karol Gunár (PhD Social Sciences) said that we didn't have to go to school that day because of the tragic disaster that had happened regarding our classmate.

I couldn't stop looking at Darinka Gunárová's arms wondering why both her arms were bandaged.

Once there was this man in Komárno and his arms had to be bandaged like that. His name was Róbert Sekule. Róbert Sekule was weird regarding sexual things because he was naughty sexually. He used to exposition himself.

Because that's what some people are like and they like to exposition themselves.

And that's what Róbert Sekule was like, too And because he was like that he used to go to the Young Craftsmen's Club every Sunday morning but in reality he didn't go there. In reality he used to go to the Klement Gottwald Park and exposition himself.

His wife's name was Júlia Sekulová and she suspected that Róbert Sekule was sexually naughty, so one day she decided to follow him to find out what this Young Craftsmen's Club was all about. And that's when she saw it. She went back home and didn't say anything to him but next Sunday, when he left home, she followed him along with some acid and when he started doing it she poured the acid on his hands and down there. You know where I mean. On his penis.

After that Róbert Sekule's arms had to be bandaged until he had an operation and then they had to be bandaged again because of the operation he had. And then he moved to Hlohovec and nothing more happened after that.

His wife went to jail regarding the acid that had burned his thing so badly that there wasn't much left to operate on but they operated anyway.

And then everyone said that at least he wouldn't be naughty any more and exposition himself and everyone admired Júlia Sekulová.

I also said so and I admired her, too.

So that's why I got so worked up regarding the bandages on Darinka Gunárová's arms and wondered what they were for. And then Karol Gunár (PhD Social Sciences) said that I should keep an eye on her because she might try to run away through the window.

That was very weird because we lived on the third floor and it's forbidden to climb out of there.

Then I looked at Darinka Gunárová and I asked her what had happened to her regarding the bandages. And she said that she had broken the window because she wanted to run away and join Tonko Szedílek.

I didn't know what to say.

So after that neither of us said anything.

Then my Dad and Karol Gunár (PhD Social Sciences) started drinking an alcoholic drink and my Mum left and went to Grandaddy's place.

I was happy that Darinka Gunárová was in our house because we could talk except that we didn't talk because Darinka Gunárová wouldn't say anything.

I didn't say anything either.

Then my Dad and Karol Gunár (PhD Social Sciences) started singing Slovak folk songs, because Slovak folk songs are the most beautiful in the world. That's what they said on TV and also at school. They said Slovak folk songs were the most beautiful because the Slovak people were the most beautiful people and everyone respected us for it.

I respect us for it, too.

And then something very weird happened. As they were singing Darinka Gunárová stuck the rubber golliwog between her knees and started squeezing it. And the rubber golliwog made a squeaking noise. The squeaking was very loud and I was frightened that the noise would upset Karol Gunár (PhD Social Sciences). And I was frightened that Karol Gunár (PhD Social Sciences) might get angry with me too, so I went to the piano room because I was happy that he was friends with my Dad now and that my Dad stopped making fun of the Communist Party and that things had turned out so well.

When I came back to the piano room Karol Gunár (PhD Social Sciences) patted me on the back and said that I was a good boy. He said that I was the best boy in the world and he patted me on the back and that made me very happy. And he said that I should join them in singing a song.

The thing is I don't like to sing very much and I'm not very good at singing because I don't know any songs except for some Christmas Carols and the song about my dear friend Augustin that goes like this:

'Oh, Duleeber Augustin, Augustin, Augustin,
Oh, Duleeber Augustin,
Alex is in.'

So I said that I couldn't sing but Karol Gunár (PhD Social Sciences) said that I should have a go anyway so I did. They kept singing a humorous song and Darinka Gunárová kept making squeaking golliwog noises.

The song they sang was this very humorous song about a woman called Katuša and how she did it with priests. I learned to sing it too because it was very humorous. And the beginning went like this:

'Katuša was a pretty maid
Always ready to get laid.
Hey ho, hey ho, what did I see through her window?
Hey ho, hey ho, I saw the chaplain on her pillow,
Hey ho, hey ho, on Katuša's pillow.'

And then we sang the whole song again except that after the chaplain this woman called Katuša did it with the priest and then the bishop and then the pope. And this is what we sang at the end of each verse: 'Hey ho, hey ho, on Katuša's pillow'.

And then suddenly this was what my Dad sang:

'Hey ho, hey ho, I saw Karol Gunár on her pillow,
Hey ho, hey ho, on Katuša's pillow.'

I got really frightened that Karol Gunár (PhD Social Sciences) might take offence but he didn't take offence because he had lots of good qualities and he said that he and my Dad should call each other by first names.

And then they started calling each other by first names and became very good friends because everything turned out so well.

After that we kept singing and they kept drinking alcoholic drinks and Karol Gunár (PhD Social Sciences) said that he would make sure that Ivana got a place at the piano school in Bratislava and that he could also get a job for Margita at the City Hall, so she could send children into children's homes if she wanted to.

And we were all very happy about that.

Only Darinka Gunárová wasn't happy, because every time we sang the humorous song about this woman called Katuša she made squeaky golliwog noises.

Karol Gunár (PhD Social Sciences) said that we should ignore her.

So we ignored her.

And then it was the evening and they went home and my Dad said that Gunár could drink like an ox, even though he was a Commie.

And he really respected him for that.

I really respected him for that, too.

But the one thing I don't get is why Darinka Gunárová never wanted to be friends with me any more, especially seeing as our families became friends and everything had turned out well.

The only thing that didn't turn out well was that Uncle Otto somehow found out what had happened and he went to see Karol Gunár (PhD Social Sciences) in the Communist Party and said that it was all Karol Gunár (PhD Social Sciences)'s fault that Tonko had died because Karol Gunár (PhD Social Sciences) could have saved his life if he'd been a decent human being.

But Karol Gunár (PhD Social Sciences) is very kind and he didn't take offence at Uncle Otto at all because he knew that Uncle Otto wasn't right in the head due to the lightning that went in at his shoulder and out of his foot, so he just called in the security man from the Reception and had him thrown out.

When Grandaddy found out what Uncle Otto had said to Karol Gunár (PhD Social Sciences) he got so badly worked up that he had to lie down propped up on four pillows and take one of those pills that you don't swallow, you just put them under your tongue. Then he pointed to the lamp and said that we were all done for and that the High Ups wouldn't let us get away with it.

And after that he started locking Uncle Otto in the back room, the one that we used as larder and that had the table with the marble top, and he shouted at him that he was as stupid as his bloody Gappy Mushrooms.

Meaning that Uncle Otto was as stupid as his Happy Mushrooms. He used to laugh at Uncle Otto because Uncle Otto always said the names of all mushrooms as if they were in Russian because he had learned all about mushrooms from this Russian teacher when he was out of his body in Balakhashka, and that's why Uncle Otto learned the names of all the mushrooms in Russian.

Except that Russian doesn't have the letter H, it only has the letter G.

So when Grandaddy got angry with Uncle Otto he used to say that he was as stupid as his Gappy Mushrooms and that it was that blood in him that was showing. Meaning the blood that Grandmummy had got from her Grandmother whose name was Eszter Csonka and who was half Hungarian, and maybe even something worse.

And that's why Grandaddy used to call him stupid Gappy Mushroom.

There was this man in Komárno whose name was Zdenko Horilla and he was the manager of a Cinema. Once he was sent to the Soviet Union regarding Friendship because back then we still had the Soviet Union so it was OK. And during Friendship they drank all sorts of Soviet alcoholic drinks and because Russian doesn't have the letter H they called him Gorilla instead of Horilla. He didn't like that at all and when they finished drinking all the Soviet alcoholic drinks he said this:

'If you call me Gorilla we will say Haharin instead of Gagarin.'

And everyone in the Soviet Union took offence because he offended the World's First Soviet Cosmonaut and when he came home he got into big trouble because he had offended them. And he couldn't be manager of the Cinema any more.

And then everyone said it served him right, even managers should keep their mouths shut in the Soviet Union.

I said so, too.

Because he shouldn't have offended the World's First Soviet Cosmonaut.

Anyway.

This Zdenko Horilla had a daughter whose name was Zdenka Horillová and she was almost the only one in Komárno who ever let old Gusto Rúhe grope her, due to being very desperate because she was very unhappy.

She was unhappy because this P.E. teacher had left her and she wanted old Gusto Rúhe to tell her if anything could be done so that he would come back to her. So she let him grope her and this is what Gusto Rúhe wrote on the tarmac:

'Sandal-mandal chamtay tsog.'

But nobody knew what this meant because everyone knew that old Gusto Rúhe was just making it up so that he could grope and that's why nobody believed that sandal-mandal chamtay tsog meant anything.

I didn't believe it either.

Zdenka Horillová was the only one who believed that it meant something and she kept trying to figure out what it meant and as she was trying to figure it out she forgot all about being unhappy regarding the P.E. teacher and married someone completely different who wasn't a P.E. teacher or any other kind of teacher at all, but a carpenter regarding antique chairs and other furnitures.

And people said that everything turned out well even though sandal-mandal chamtay tsog didn't mean anything.

I said so, too.

But anyway, I'd like to know what sort of rubbish this sandal-mandal chamtay tsog was because old Gusto Rúhe just makes things up and people believe him because they have no idea.

Anyway.

But when he told my fortune he said this thing about the Cemetery Book, so I have to be very careful because you never know what might happen because he might even put a spell on me like he did on Erik Rak if I don't write the Cemetery Book.

When I've finished writing this I will write about how he put a spell on Erik Rak because I forgot again because sometimes I forget things because I have lots of things to worry about, because I'm not like those people who don't have anything to worry about. Usually I have lots of things to worry about but now that I'm being a writer due to my rear-view mirror I don't have as many things to worry about as usual when I'm hard-working regarding cardboard.

Because I'm always very hard-working regarding cardboard.

Other people are not so hard-working. Alf Névéry, for example, never worked hard so he didn't have anything to worry about and all he did was sleep all day long and keep his lights on all night long and look at *The Safe City* by Uncle Otto and sometimes he would give me Karlsbad Wafers.

Because the one thing I don't get is how someone can stand it not being hard-working. I couldn't stand it because I'm very hard-working.

Sometimes people tell me to stop being so hard-working and I always tell them that I'm hard-working and that's why I work hard. Because if I were lazy I wouldn't be working. That's a fact and it goes without saying, right?

Right.

I've been hard-working ever since I left school and I stopped going there because I left school. Some people said they wouldn't mind staying at school and they stayed there because they wanted to. But I said that I wouldn't go to school any more because I wanted to be hard-working.

Darinka Gunárová, for example, kept going to school, but not for much longer, because she married the fat slob Manica even though he was really nasty, because he didn't work and had long hair and she was only sixteen years old.

That made Karol Gunár (PhD Social Sciences) very unhappy but there was nothing he could do about it because Darinka Gunárová said that she was going to have a baby and that's when you have to get married, because that's the law. So she got married, but then it turned out that it wasn't true and she didn't have a baby, but she was already married to that fat slob Manica who kept shouting at me like this:

'Everybody thinks
Samko Tále stinks.'

Anyway.

Later she got divorced and left to emigrate to America. But that was very bad for Karol Gunár (PhD Social Sciences), because people might have thought that he was fond of America even though he was PhD Social Sciences, because Darinka Gunárová left to emigrate there.

That made him very unhappy and once when I went to see him to report everything he said he had something to tell me and this was what he said then:

'It's all my fault.'

Meaning not that it was all my fault but that it was all his fault, he just said my fault because he was talking of himself, but what he meant was that it was his fault that Darinka Gunárová left to emigrate.

Because it goes without saying that she didn't leave because of me because we were just classmates and she married the nasty fat slob Manica, not me. She couldn't have married me because I've never married anyone, because I don't have time for silly things like marrying because I have lots of things to do due to being hard-working.

Besides I never did anything with Darinka Gunárová because she was Class Prefect and I wasn't Class Prefect because I wasn't.

The only time I did anything with Darinka Gunárová was when I lent her my handkerchief when she was being sick after eating green beans that were grown in the school garden even though it was forbidden. And then she was sick in the school yard and everyone ran away from her.

I was the only one who didn't run away from her.

I gave her my handkerchief because she didn't have one and I did because I always have one. She never gave it back to me but I didn't report her because I didn't need it and now I'm so well-off that I could easily buy two hundred handkerchiefs if I felt like it. But I don't feel like it, because what's the point of having two hundred handkerchiefs, right?

Right.

So it goes without saying that it wasn't my fault that she left to emigrate and that it was somebody else's fault, even though Karol Gunár (PhD Social Sciences) believed that it was his fault, but I don't get it and I will never understand what gave him this idea because he's always been very kind and has always been helping everyone.

Karol Gunár (PhD Social Sciences) had lots of good qualities.

For example, he taught me this humorous song about the woman called Katuša who did all sorts of sexual things with priests.

Once I sang this song to Alf Névéry because I thought that he might want to learn it too so that at last he might have something humorous to say but he didn't want to learn it and instead he asked where I had learned it so I told him that I had learned it from Karol Gunár (PhD Social Sciences) after everything had turned out well.

I thought that it would make him laugh but he didn't laugh even though the song is very humorous especially where it says about how she did it with the Pope. That's really very humorous.

But it didn't make Alf Névéry laugh at all and he didn't even give me any Karlsbad Wafers, he just stared at Uncle Otto's *The Safe City* and then the next day I found him dead.

I have no idea why he died because nobody has ever told me, so I really have no way of telling why he died because nobody in Komárno or anywhere else in the world knew why.

Sometimes I think that he died because he wasn't humorous at all because people should be humorous. And people should also have a healthy life of style and drink lots of yoghurt and take plenty of exercise in the fresh air.

Because yoghurt is really very good for you.

Anyway.

also available from the Garnett Press

Д. Рейфилд, О. Макарова (ред.). Дневник Алексея Сергеевича Суворин (*Dairy of Aleksei Suvorin, the 19th C. Russian magnate, in Russian*). 1999, pp xl+666 ISBN 0 9535878 0 0   £20.00

D. Rayfield, J Hicks, O Makarova, A. Pilkington (editors) *The Garnett Book of Russian Verse. An Anthology with English Prose Translation* 2000, 748 pp. ISBN 0 9535878 2 7 £25.00

Donald Rayfield, editor in chief (with Rusudan Amirejibi, Shukia Apridonidze, Laurence Broers, Levan Chkhaidze, Ariane Chanturia, Tina Margalitadze) *A Comprehensive Georgian-English Dictionary*, 2006. 2 vols. pp xl + 172. ISBN 978-0-9535878-3-4   £75.00
(*a few seconds [8 replacement pages inserted in volume 2] are available at £40.00*)

Peter Pišt'anek, translated by Peter Petro. *Rivers of Babylon* 2007. pp 259. ISBN 978-0-9535878-4-1   £12.99

Peter Pišt'anek, translated by Peter Petro *The Wooden Village* (*Rivers of Babylon 2*) 2008. pp 206. ISBN 978-0-9535878-5-8   £11.99

Peter Pišt'anek, translated by Peter Petro *The End of Freddy* (*Rivers of Babylon 3)* 2008. pp 206. ISBN 978-0-9535878-6-5   £13.99

Nikolai Gogol, Marc Chagall *Dead Souls* , a new translation by Donald Rayfield, *with 96 engravings and 12 vignettes reproduced from the 1948 Tériade edition* 2008. pp366. Limited to 1500 copies, large format on heavy art paper. ISBN 978-0-9535878-7-2 £29.99

Donald Rayfield *The Literature of Georgia — A History*, 3rd revised, expanded edition. 2010. pp 366 ISBN 978-0-9535878-8-9   £25.00

forthcoming
in 2011:
Otar Chiladze *Avelum* (the fifth novel by Georgia's greatest modern novelist)

to buy our books from Queen Mary Online Store: *go to* **https://eshop.qmul.ac.uk**
then click **Product Catalogue,** *then* **Books,** *then* **Garnett Press Books,**
or contact:
d.rayfield@qmul.ac.uk
or write to:
Garnett Press, School of Languages, Literature and Film, Queen Mary University of London, Mile End Road, London E1 4NS, UK